D1572462

OFFICIALLY
DISCARDED

The
Dispossessed

A NOVEL BY

Don Carpenter

|||

cop. 1

NORTH POINT PRESS
San Francisco · 1986

FOR LEW WELCH, ON BRAZEN WING

The Dispossessed

Just at the moment of dawn, Milos appeared out of the darkness at the edge of the town square and walked toward the depot. Above the town the mountain stood green in the morning light, which was just touching the tiled roof of the former train station. Milos loved and hated the mountain, and felt he could not exist out of its influence. Inside the depot there was a light, as usual. The early morning woman was in there getting ready for the day, counting out the money, heating the water in the espresso machine, cutting up the fruit for salads. Soon the trucks would come with the bundles of newspapers, and then soon after that the place would open for business. But Milos would not be welcome inside. No coffee for Milos, even if he offered to pay. Dressed in several layers of coats, shirts, pants, parts of blanket, and his greasy old fatigue hat, Milos began his day's work, pacing up and down in front of the now blank-eyed windows of the depot, grinning and gesticulating, shouting in English, French, or Czech. It did not matter what he shouted. There was no one to hear him except the old lady inside, who was not afraid of him anyway.

The town had been there for more than a hundred years, beginning back in the days of the gold rush as the millsite for cutting down, sawing, and trimming giant redwoods to provide lumber for the city twenty miles south, on the other side of the big bay. There had been a railroad once, to haul the lumber to the scows that sailed it across the bay, the tracks running down through the salt marsh below the town. But the railroad tracks had been pulled up, and the alluvial gravels of the right-of-way had been covered in asphalt for a bike path. Most of the mountain was a federal park. The town was now a suburb, and most, but not all, of its people commuters to the city.

Milos was dirty, bearded, wild-eyed, and looked like an anarchist with a bomb. He liked to frighten the commuters as they crossed the square with their satchels, cartons of coffee, and folded newspapers, hurrying for their seats on the buses. Always hurrying. The same people, morning after morning, always late, always in a hurry, scurrying around Milos without meeting his eye while the bus made awful noises at the bottom of the square.

"Après moi, nada!" Milos shouted at his first commuter of the day. The man wore a dark suit and a tan raincoat, even though it was a clear day and probably would not rain for another six months.

"Ve bo't oberdressed!" Milos shouted at the dodging man.

The depot opened, and the rhythms of the morning thickened. Morning customers, commuters, schoolchildren, other town square hangers-out, depot regulars, cars, buses, dogs, seagulls attracted by the smell of food, and a congress of crows who came through cawing and crying nearly every morning. Milos thought the crows were his spiritual enemies and he often chased them, waving his stick, knowing he looked foolish. But of course no one would dare to speak to him or make fun of him. He was too crazy. He savored his craziness. He knew he was not really crazy. This was just how it had all broken down, these clothes, his bedroll hidden away among the redwoods, this plaza for his stage. He had first come here when the police of another town had picked him up and brought him, leaving him off in front of the depot and telling him he would not be welcome back in their town. It was a common practice.

But it was not to be an easy day for Milos. Today the river of life would change, fluctuate, meander into a new channel. Today there would come a new crazy man to the town square.

THERE were plenty of odd characters hanging around the square already, but no one, Milos prided himself, as crazy as himself. There were several men who did not seem able to get over the war or their military experiences, wearing uniforms they had made for themselves out of parts of real uniforms, a beret here, a bit of camouflage there, dark patches where stripes had been. Some of these were paid by the government for their disabilities; others had never actually been in the service, but seemed to miss it anyway. There were women, too, not quite bag ladies, not quite anything else.

It was from among these that Milos got most of his money. When he had money he would ask people to go into the depot for him and get coffee or a sandwich. Many days he got no money at all. He was not above eating scraps and drinking cold coffee dregs left by someone more affluent, but no one ever saw him do it, and so far he had only been caught once stealing vegetables from a midnight garden, and that once the woman had only pounded on the window. Milos had fled and hidden in some bushes, but the police never came, so she hadn't called them. Milos thanked her for that—and continued, from time to time, taking things from her garden: tomatoes, zucchini, string beans, apples. He would eat these raw, and from time to time he would have agonizing gut problems. But that was Karma.

Today he got a quick dollar from the tall woman with the camera, who also let him finish her *caffe latte*.

"Ah, *caffe latte! Caffe latte!*" he exclaimed, gesturing with the big plastic cup, grinning to show he was happy. The tall woman with the camera was one of those who felt they were contributing to society by helping the less fortunate, although, some might speculate, in some ways it would be difficult to find anybody less fortunate than this poor woman. Milos hid the dollar away. If he got another one and then fifty cents, he would buy a turkey sandwich, which would last him two days. But enough about food! Damn food! We must have it, but damn it all, anyway!

It was going to be a rare summer day, without any fog or wind, one of a string of nice warm days, making the town seem like a paradise, for it never really got too hot in the summer or too cold in winter. The worst thing that had ever happened to the place was a flood a couple of years before, when all the creeks that came down the mountain went angry with rain and coldly flooded the square. Milos spent a few weeks in the city, until all the mud and wreckage had been cleared away. But today was already getting nice and warm.

Tim, the manager of the depot, came out the back door and stood in the shade of the building, looking at Milos and the others who were beginning to gather, standing alone or sitting on the old benches. Tim would have loved to have gotten rid of all these bums, but they had been around longer than he had, and so that was that. Tim was a tall soft-looking man of forty, whose sandy hair was receding, and whose pale blue eyes met the snapping black eyes of Milos without expression. Tim and Milos did not speak. They had not spoken since the day, months ago, when Milos had screamed at the old woman inside the place and thus been kicked out. Eighty-sixed.

But Tim had more on his mind than just Milos, or even the problems of running the depot at something like a profit. He was worried this morning about one of the women who worked for him. Barry was her name, Barry Latimer, a jazz singer by desire, a kitchen worker by trade. She had not shown up for work the night before, and Tim was more upset than worried. Barry had been on the edge of getting fired when Tim turned her around. Or at least he thought he had turned her around.

When she had first come to work Barry had been lazy and slow, often late, phoning in with excuses, typical of the person who thinks she is too good for the job. She was very pretty, with large dark eyes and a slender lazy figure. She was twenty-nine, and had not made a great success of her singing. Tim had taken her aside and told her over coffee that she had better pay attention to business or lose her job. She broke down and cried, which Tim had not expected be-·cause she had seemed tougher than that, but things had been piling up on her, an accompanist had accused her of being a prima donna and quit, her boyfriend had borrowed her last hundred dollars and run off, singing jobs had grown scarcer and scarcer to the point where she was beginning to wonder if it wasn't time to throw in the towel.

Then they really had a talk, and Tim told her about himself, his plans for his own restaurant someday, how he had already owned one place and lost it to his dissolving marriage; and then she told him about her life in music, the Berklee School in Boston, the years in New York, then Los Angeles, and now here out in the middle of the sticks.

Tim grinned. He liked her now. She had spirit. "I guess kitchen work isn't very interesting to anybody," he said.

"But if I take the job I should do the work," she said, and he truly thought they had had a meeting of the minds on this. Barry had improved from that day on, and the other workers noticed, liked her better themselves, and things had been going along fine. Tim had really been happy about it.

When she had not showed up for work the night before, they called Tim at home, and he in turn called Barry, but got no answer. He thought about calling her now. He glanced at the big town clock on the edge of the square, and then grinned to himself. That clock had not told the correct time in years.

She did not answer her telephone. Tim was disturbed and a little angry. He hung up the wall telephone in the tiny kitchen space and watched the old woman, Dorothy, as she bent over the cutting board out behind the counter making a sandwich, her old brown hands seeming to move slowly but the sandwich building quickly, avocado, tomato, jack cheese, and alfalfa sprouts, *whick* with the big wickedly sharp butcher knife, as she talked over her shoulder continuously to the Persian girl who was at the espresso machine scalding milk in a brass pot to make *latte*. They were talking about cats, specifically, two kittens that Fahima wanted to give away before she and her husband Hassan went back to Iran to become revolutionaries. Kittens. Who shall have the kittens? They must go to good homes, homes where they will have company and good food, love and medical care.

A motley row of morning customers waited variously at the high glassed-in counter, examining the displayed pastries, carrot cakes, bagels, croissants, and pies. Tim moved out of the kitchen and around the counter, still thinking about Barry Latimer, songstress. A burst of hard laughter came from the old lady. What had Fahima said?

"We could bring kittens in box, and take them out on square," she had said, and the old woman had laughed.

"Some of those guys out there'd cook 'em an' eat 'em!"

Tim had to laugh himself, and just then one of what he called "the irregulars"—to distinguish the nuts on the square from the regular, desirable, moneyed customers—popped in through the back entrance onto the square, saw Tim and hesitated, finally darting into the toilet. He was a little guy called Nifty Nick, one of the vets, dressed in filthy camouflage, his hair, beard, and eyes wild, his little red mouth revealing jagged dirty teeth. He was not exactly eighty-six, but he seemed to know that Tim did not want him taking up table space. Tim sighed. It was a large part of his role as manager to distinguish between the sane and the crazy, a job he felt unsuited for, since often he felt everybody was crazy, especially himself.

Tim's own downfall had been as trite as it had been rapid. He had made the classical mistake of going into business with 1) A man who did not understand business, particularly the food business and 2) who was his father-in-law. When the breakup came he found his soon-to-be exwife controlling 75% of the business. Tim went on a monumental drinking bout with his brother and ended up managing the depot, a daily waystop for commuters, crazy people, and the floating population of the southern half of the county.

The tall, very beautiful Persian girl smiled at him across the pastries and he smiled back at her, warming instantly. Of course he loved her. Everybody who knew her loved her. She had the kind of rich aristocratic beauty you never get to see in places like this. Fahima's family had been wealthy landowners once, and still had money. She had been formally cut off when, coming to America at eighteen, she had moved into a slum neighborhood in Boston and married Hassan, whose family were, frankly, gamblers and wastrels. Fahima told Tim, "It was best day of my life!" Happily she found the worst job she could, and when she and Hassan came west to another school she happily found this job at the depot, bad pay and poor working conditions—just what she liked.

When Fahima got back to Iran she planned to go to work in a factory, to help spread the revolution. Her mother, living in Paris, and her father, still in Tehran, thought she was crazy to go back. So did Tim.

Fahima smiled at him with warmth and deep understanding. He was a nice man, but he did not understand the revolution.

The old woman had a better attitude. "You win your revolution and then come back to us," Dorothy told her once.

"Oh, no!" Fahima had said. "Not to America!"

"It's not such a bad place, is it?" As she talked, Dorothy reduced a cantaloupe into small orange cubes and dumped them in with the rest of the cut-up fruit. "I never been anyplace else, but I like it here just fine."

"Is wonderful place," Fahima said. "Too wonderful."

"Yeah, I guess we should all be out doin' somethin'." So much for the revolution.

Then, a minor incident, the kind that happened almost every day—an almost-but-not-quite situation. The man waiting for his espresso was a stocky tense-looking person who came in once a week or so and always kidded the help if they were anything like pretty—always wore dark green matching pants and shirt, uniformlike but without any identifying name on the back or over the pocket. Now he was kidding Fahima, who kept downcast eyes through it all. Tim watched from a distance, wanting to take the guy outside and punch him out, or at the very least eighty-six him. But why? Lots of men kidded the good-looking girls, and this guy said things no worse than most. In fact, it was not the words he used at all, but the tension he was obviously under. Clearly the man hated women. As he kidded, his tense white lips betrayed his true feelings, and his significant pose as he ostentatiously dropped a quarter ringing into the tip jar drove Tim almost frantic with the desire to punch the guy.

But Tim controlled himself, and the man walked slowly out onto the square sipping his too-hot espresso in its white plastic cup, his eyes darting around at the various people. Should he sit among the creeps today? Couple of them were pretty interesting characters. The little guy in the camouflage fatty-gyues had aced a number of Vietnamese, for example, using his brightsharp bayonet blade to sever ears, fingers, little girl breasts; had shoved that blade into many a gookish gut—worth talking to. But the little fucker regretted everything, and if you talked to him about it he'd shut right up.

The guy in green, whose name was Dick, sat on the edge of one of the concrete raised flower beds, the flowers sad among the beer bottles and cigarette butts. He did not have a call for another hour yet. He worked for Fix-M-Up, driving all over the southern end of the county repairing whatever, as he put it, keeping his ears open, picking up bits and pieces, acquiring knives for his collection. He had over eight hundred knives at home. Most of them were ordinary knives, kitchen knives, old ones and new ones, but he had some Randalls and some other custom knives as well. He loved knives, it went without saying, but what he loved most was thinking about sliding those blades into some human guts. He had not been to war. He had been too young, worse luck.

The sun warm on his face he smiled at Milos, the crazy one with the stick.

"You ever stab anybody, you little fucker?" he asked pleasantly. Milos' face darkened.

"You are bad man! Bad man!" Milos shouted. He moved away from the guy in green, furious. What right did this crazy man have talking to him? What kind of world was it, anyway?

H E was first noticed by the group of heavy thinkers who hung out in front of the depot, on the street side. Across the street was an island of redwood trees edged by white curbing and containing a tall flagpole on a wide concrete base. On authorized days an American flag hung from the staff among the redwood branches, and every Christmas the Lions Club put up strings of colored lights. One of these strings, placed by nobody knew who, proved out of reach when it came time to bring the lights down, and so it still hung there in the foliage, blue, red, and yellow bulbs grim with dust and dirt.

Beneath them, half on the curbing at the west end of the tree island, sat a man, crosslegged, with a big open satchel bulging with goods, among them brightly colored yarns and sharp plastic needles. On his lap the man had something he was busy knitting. He was not a stranger. All three of the deep thinkers that morning had seen him many times before, often inside the depot early in the morning, when he would hang over the counter and burble at the old woman as she got things ready. In a police description, the man would have been called black, but he was very light-skinned, with a blaze of acne scars across his cheeks, and resented being identified with any racial group. He was androgynous as well, with a voluptuous womanly figure, except, of course, for his chest. He was considered, until today, to be a mere simpleton.

Now here he was, knitting a shawl or something, sitting on the curb with his legs out in the street where a car turning tightly might hit him.

The three men, with their plastic cups of coffee, commented on him.

"Another nut," said Victor. Victor was himself a bulky man with a large stomach and a long black beard, dressed in a derby, railroad coveralls and a shoulder bag filled with cameras and equipment, plus a bunch of celery, from which he would now and again remove a stalk and feed it into his mouth. Victor was on a diet.

"A nigger, a faggot, and a nut," said Zeno, not unkindly. Zeno was a big handsome man dressed in a green polo shirt with a darker green alligator over the pocket, pale denims and slick white and green Adidas, though Zeno never ran. Adidas were fashionable, and the green and white ones were the most expensive. Zeno leaned on his maroon Mercedes sedan, which he parked in front of the depot each morning for about an hour, before going to his office in the city. He worked for the leader of a gigantic semireligious cult, and busied himself teaching cult leaders the intricacies of life on tax exempt status. Zeno was not himself a believer.

"Geez, I wonder what he's makin' there," said Piper, whose shock of white hair above a bulging forehead gave the impression of intellectuality until Piper opened his mouth. Piper wore a grey sweatsuit and Earth shoes, false teeth, and a nervous blink. Piper was a sculptor, had a studio and everything, but made his living selling sets of cookware and kitchen knives, somehow conveying to his potential customers the idea that these goods had been stolen and were thus a bargain. They were not stolen, but bought wholesale in the city. He had actually been a thief at one time, but the risks had been too great. Then he became a beautician in Los Angeles, and now this. Piper was a strong advocate of Zen Buddhism, about which he knew almost nothing.

"Looks like he's making a rug," Victor said.

"Won't the cops get on his case?" Piper asked.

But Zeno wanted to get back to their conversation. "Be that as it may," he said. "The heart and soul of existentialism died with Camus."

"I disagree! I disagree!" said Piper, who also fancied himself as a standup comedian. "The essence of existentialism is tied up in the essence of Zen, that's the tradition."

"My God, what stupidity," said Victor, who was from a wealthy family and had a law degree, although he did not practice much. "You guys kill me."

And on they went, meaninglessly, enjoying the coming heat of the morning and their coffee. Across the wide street the new nut sat quietly knitting.

Soon a potbellied man in a white shirt and a bow tie came out of the stationery store and went up to the man knitting. The three in front of the depot paused in their conversation and watched. The potbellied man was shaking his finger at the seated man, and then went back into his store.

"Probably told him to take a hike," Zeno said.

"He's not hurting anybody," Piper said.

"He's a saint," Victor said ironically, but later his remark was taken as prophetic.

Several customers of the commuter type complained loudly inside the depot about the man, until finally Tim came out and looked. He could see no harm being done, so he went back into the depot and back to putting away crates of vegetables and fruit. He had to check each new load carefully, because sometimes lately the produce had been poor in quality, particularly the carrots, which were getting too big and tough. After a while somebody came in and said, "The cops are out there."

Yes. One of the town's white police cars was pulled up in front of the seated man, whose name was Valerie but who actively resented accusations of homosexuality. The short young policeman with the

southern accent was polite to him. There had been complaints from
merchants. He would have to move. It was a nice day, wasn't it?
Valerie finally stood up, stuffing his work into his bag, and allowed
the little policeman to escort him across to the curb in front of the
depot. With a wave for everyone watching, the policeman then
drove off, and Valerie went back out and sat down again.

"This could be the start of something big," said Zeno.

BY noon it was hot. The square was busy with kids on skateboards and bicycles, lunching workers from the surrounding shops, idlers catching the sun, mothers with their little children out for a stroll in this unusually fine weather. The normal summer pattern of morning and evening chill fog had not taken over yet, somehow, and everyone seemed bucked up, expectant, ready for something wonderful to happen.

Inside the depot things were slow, and Tim took this opportunity to telephone Barry Latimer. Again, she did not answer, and again Tim, with a sinking heart, thought about either going up to her place himself or calling the police. But why call the police? She was just unreliable, that was all. And he really did not want to go up there. Then the microwave oven went on the fritz, and Tim forgot about Barry Latimer.

Valerie sat quietly in the wonderful sunshine knitting his lovely bed cover, which was to be a gigantic brown and green and scarlet mandala, brown for God, green for Nature, and scarlet for Mankind, harmony and disharmony engaged in an endless beauty battle, right there on top of somebody's bed. It would certainly not go on Valerie's spartan bed, with its blue blanket and single hard pillow. Valerie lived in what had been a chickenhouse, out behind the home of his benefactor, an old retired Marine gunnery sergeant who liked his pogey on a regular basis and did not mind the few bucks a month Valerie cost him. And after all, Valerie worked around the place and really earned his keep. Perhaps the bed cover was for Harry, the retired Marine. Perhaps not.

Before, Valerie's life had been strange and frightening, and when his mind traveled backward into it he could feel again the terrible belly terror that chased him dark into the mist, where he could not remember. Living with greasy little Jake, who claimed to love him but made him dress as a woman and walk the streets of the city. For fifteen dollars Valerie would guide the customer to a dark alleyway to park. Seldom did the customer know he was a man, but sometimes that's what they wanted and Valerie would have to cooperate. Ugh. Ugh. The whole thing had been disgusting.

Here came the policeman again. What a bother! Valerie got to his feet as the little cop opened his door and grimly got out.

"I thought we had an understanding," said the cop in a voice of authority.

"I'm not doing any harm," Valerie said loudly. There were people watching all over.

"Well, I'm going to have to haul your ass away," the policeman said.

"I don't want to go away. I want to stay here. I am not doing anybody any harm. This is a public place."

"You're sittin' in the street, complaints are comin' in."

The old woman came up to them, her hands under her red apron. "What's goin' on?" she asked the policeman.

"Oh, hi, Dorothy," the policeman said.

"I know this guy," she said. "He ain't doin' no harm."

"I gotta do what I gotta do, nonetheless," said the policeman.

"Where you takin' him?" Dorothy asked, as the policeman herded Valerie into the backseat of the white police car.

"Just for a little ride," said the policeman.

Dorothy shrugged and ambled back to the depot. The police car drove off to faint cheers from the various sunworshippers. As soon as the white car was out of sight, Milos popped into view, shouting and gesticulating, standing on the corner by the public drinking fountain. A woman was holding her little boy up to get a drink, but

Milos upset her, and she went off before the little boy had satisfied himself. The little boy gave Milos a dirty look, which Milos returned with interest.

"Baby rats, everywhere baby rats," he said to no one.

By two in the afternoon Valerie was back from his ride up to the next town, settled into place, and once again knitting. After a while a young girl came up to him and said, "I think you have great courage."

"Thank you," Valerie said with dignity.

Some others came up to him during the course of the day and in one way or the other, congratulated him on his courage. He liked that. He had not thought about courage, but it *was* courage, wasn't it?

Among those who came up to him was Milos, who made several frantic sorties halfway or less across the street, always turning back angrily because he had forgotten what he wanted to say, but finally standing in front of the crosslegged Valerie hopping and waving his stick.

"You get out of here! This is my place!"

"Oh, go fuck yourself," Valerie said. "I'm not afraid of you, crazy man."

"You crazy too!"

"And you're another damn cop," said Valerie.

Bested and baffled, Milos retreated to the square, and sat by himself, glowering, thoughts cascading through his mind in three languages, a flow of words like bright blue electricity.

WHEN the siren was first heard everyone looked expectantly over toward the crosslegged Valerie, but Tim knew beforehand somehow that the police car would go right past the square and turn up the hill, disappearing among the trees. When that happened, Tim felt a wave of despair, for he knew in his Irish heart that the siren was for Barry Latimer. He looked helplessly around his depot domain as if searching for escape. Everything seemed normal. They heard twenty sirens a day in there, police, fire trucks from the station around the corner, the harsh painbright sirens of the ambulances when some poor soul fell down and could not get up or could not breathe or lay bleeding. Dorothy was chatting with Fahima, both smiling in their red aprons; coffee drinkers sat at the tables against the windows, a few cups and plates left at tables where the customers hadn't bused for themselves. Tim, without thinking, moved around the room picking up, straightening, wiping tabletops, his heart frozen with the awful knowledge he could not speak of because it really wasn't knowledge but intuition, and he would be laughed at when Barry came in lazy through the double front door, an ironic grin of apology on her sweet not quite young face. Ah, but he knew this would not happen.

Four hours passed before the police car slid to a quiet stop in front of the depot, once again paying no attention to Valerie on his spot. The early shift was long gone and the square crowded with kids, all-day hangers-on, and the first of the evening's steady drinkers. Tim was almost due to leave himself. He was taking his present wife and her two daughters to dinner that night, a special dinner before one of the daughters went south for her summer job at the beach. But the feeling of dread would not go away. He kept busying himself around the place until, as he knew they would, the police came in, sober faced and looking a little over their heads.

The tall policeman took off his glasses, which disturbed Tim more than anything that had happened before.

"What's the matter?" he asked the tall cop.

The tall cop ran his hand through his thinning hair, and grinned with embarrassment. "You have an employee named Barry Latimer?" he asked, although he knew the answer. Tim nodded grimly, his face heating up, his muscles tensing.

"Yes," he said.

"I have some, well, I wonder if you would come with us?"

"Come with you?"

"There has been a killing, Tim. At her place. We need somebody to identify the remains."

"Oh, my God," Tim said. His numb fingers fumbled with his apron strings. They were already outside when he finally got the apron off, and he sat in the back of the police car with the apron wadded in his big hands.

They pulled up in front of the house where Barry rented the basement apartment. There were several city and county cars parked at odd angles in front of the place, and one big white ambulance. Before getting out of the car the tall cop turned half around to Tim and said apologetically, "It's going to be rough, Tim. Pretty fucking rough."

Pretty fucking rough was an inadequate description of what Tim was led into. Police scientists and plainclothes officers stopped what they were doing and watched Tim's reaction to the scene. His face was white with strain and his lips tense, but in his eyes was an ancestral hardness, and he needed that hardness.

Barry had not just been killed. Clearly she had been chased and hacked at with a knife, finally caught, killed, stabbed repeatedly, and then hacked into pieces. Blood was everywhere, huge obscene pools, dark spatters and stains, pathetic handprints. There was a sharp metallic smell. And the smell of shit. In a corner of the room by the records, as if it had rolled there, was Barry's head. Her eyes were open, blood all over her face and in her hair, blood clotted in one eye socket, the other eye calm. Her lips were slightly parted. Tim could see pink blood on her teeth.

"That's—that's," his throat seized up, and he coughed harshly. "That's Barry," he said finally.

The policemen all watched him.

Then, outside once more in the unbelievably sweet fresh air, a depression settled over Tim. But he was also hardening. Somebody had done this. Somebody had gotten inside, invited or not, and killed her, not just killed her but savaged her, some mad animal. Tim thought at once of all the nuts around the town square and wondered if it could have bee one of them. He would find out. He would find out just exactly who had done this, yes he would. . .

"I'm sorry," the tall policeman with the glasses said. "We'll have to wait for the sheriff. He's coming himself."

Tim said dully, "Why? But why? Why would anybody do such a thing?" Abruptly, he vomited. Bent over, retching, he apologized. The tall cop said a couple of cops had vomited too.

Wiping his mouth on the apron wadded in his hand, Tim wondered if he was himself a suspect. Of course he was. Everybody would be, until this thing got solved. But he did not care. In his mind he would see, forever, that one eye, calmly staring at nothing.

THE sky was just going from grey to blue in the east when the old woman, Dorothy, came down the one hundred redwood steps that led from her tiny apartment, and then down the street to the depot. She wore two sweaters, even though it was not cold, and hugged herself as she walked. She was slightly stoned, as she was every morning. There was no one on the street or on the square when she let herself into the depot. She thought people would start showing up early because the weather was so good. The night before, she had gone to bed early without watching the news, and she did not know about Barry Latimer until Fahima and her husband Hassan came in at six-thirty.

Hassan was twenty-six, handsome in a dashing Errol-Flynn way, but already beginning to get a little bald and a little soft around the middle. Hassan had an easy smile, but this morning he looked grim. Fahima looked furious. Rapidly, interrupting each other, they told Dorothy what they knew, and as they were doing this, the man came with the morning's fresh newspapers, and they looked at Barry's latest publicity photograph on the front page under the caption: SLAIN SINGER.

Dorothy sat down and cried for a few minutes, blowing her nose and wiping her eyes on the paper napkins Fahima gave her. But her tears did not last long. She had only known Barry a short time. "But I kinda liked her," she said.

"Man who kill her must be very sick," Hassan said. Often he drove his wife to work and sat drinking coffee and reading the paper before going off to his own job as a computer programmer. Now he stood, not knowing what to do with his hands.

"Sick all right," his wife said coldly.

"It's gonna be awful here today," Dorothy said. She looked out the windows overlooking the square. "I don't see any of the crazies yet. Maybe this thing scared 'em off."

Throughout the morning inside the depot everyone talked about the murder, those who had known Barry sometimes crying openly, sometimes cursing and shouting, sometimes just stunned by the news and unable to face it. Some laughed and tried to be gay, but that didn't work. When the television cameras appeared outside, many went out to watch the reporters being taped in front of the depot, and some of these were interviewed on camera. People were gathering just to look at the place where Barry had worked and soon the traffic was heavy with sightseers. Two policemen had to park their car and direct traffic. Slowly, reluctantly, the mood changed from tragic to festive.

By the time Tim arrived from the sheriff's office, where he had made and signed a formal statement, the area was crowded and busy, the depot crowded, business brisk, and the regulars all shunted off to corners while laughing, talking, gesticulating strangers everywhere took charge. Television crews and single reporters with tape recorders roamed the depot and the square looking for information. There were rumors of plainclothes cops and much talk of fears of more killing. It all disgusted Tim, whose normal day off it was, but who came to work anyway because he knew that at least one and probably more of his employees would not be able to work today. He was right, and most of the day he spent doing the most menial, least attractive jobs around the place.

Tim felt disgusted, depressed and most of all, guilty. He did not know why he should, but the plainclothes deputy who had taken his statement said it happene all the time. "We'll get a lot of confessions to this thing," he had said. "The uglier the crime, the more we get." But this did not help Tim with his feelings. The night before he had sobbed helplessly in his wife's arms, and lying awake at three in the morning, he had suffered the horrible thought that maybe he had killed Barry himself and hidden the information in his unconscious. But he had to smile grimly. Next he would be confessing.

Tim was in the slot taking coffee orders when the guy in green came in, his crooked smile hostile as usual.

"Guess we lost one, huh?" he grinned at Tim. Tim wanted to punch the man, who seemed to be having a merry old time for himself.

"I guess so," Tim said.

"I'll have an egg salad sandwich, to go, and a big coffee," said the guy in green. Fahima began to make the sandwich and Tim poured the coffee.

"I guess you better count your knives," the guy said, grinning.

"What do you mean?" Fahima asked him. She was holding the big knife ready to slice the sandwich in half.

"I mean, maybe one of 'em's missing," the guy said.

Fahima cut the sandwich angrily. When she met the guy's eyes, he winked at her triumphantly. Tim swallowed his bile, took the man's money. When the man left Tim and Fahima exchanged deep looks of understanding.

"That guy gets my goat," Tim said.

"Mine, too," said Fahima.

The guy in green leaned on the front fender of his truck, parked out front, and ate his sandwich. Like a circus out here today, lotsa high life. Pretty soon one of the local cops who was around came up to him.

"How's it going, Dick?" the cop asked.

"Hell of a deal, huh?"

The cop looked around. "You think one of these people did it?"

"You workin' on the case?"

The cop grinned flatly. "Everybody's workin' on it. We rolled up there late yesterday, Jesus, you should have seen it."

"Please, not while I'm eating."

"You wouldn't eat for a while, I guarantee you."

"Quite a mess, huh?"

Soon the cop went away and Dick finished his sandwich. It was good. He liked egg salad with a lot of mayonnaise and pepper, never mind the God damned sprouts they sprinkled all over everything. What she looked like. He hadn't done it, but he could imagine what it must have been like for the joker who did. Fear like vanilla ice-cream. Fear but no screams, he knew that girl, she wouldn't scream, she'd cuss and fight, but not scream. She'd be tough till she saw the blade and then she'd know this was no silly shit but for real. Cuts. Cuts, burns and bruises . . .

He straightened up and ambled over to the big outside trash can in its heavy rock container. Rock so that the drunks and kids wouldn't tip it over, or the dogs in the night. He put his hands on his hips and looked at the small clusters of people standing around. Innocent, ignorant. They did not know. They could not possibly understand any part of it. The release. The release from humanity, to be pure animal. That must be something, he mused. He sipped the last of his coffee and threw the plastic cup into the trash container. He cleared his throat and was about to spit a good long one when he saw the cop again, talking to a couple guys. Dainty as a maiden, he spit into the trash. Mustn't spit on the sidewalk, naughty naughty . . .

On the fringes of the crowd Valerie was furious. There were people standing where he usually liked to sit, people all over the place, disturbing his day. He did not know what to do. He was sorry for the poor girl, of course, but she hadn't been killed around here, so everyone should go home now. But they did not go, and the crowd changed, enlarged, got smaller, then swelled again, until finally

Valerie got on the bus and left the area for the day, not having gotten a thing done.

The next day things were the same, and so Valerie did not even bother to get mad, but just got back on the bus and went away. But by the third day, although the crowds were still around, although not as much, Valerie just simply walked up to his favorite spot, said, "Excuse me," as politely as possible, and sat down, crosslegged. He opened his bag, took out his piece, spread it over his legs and began work for the day. The sun was hot on his nearly shaved head, the way he liked it, and the needles clicked reassuringly.

Soon there was a space around Valerie, and not long after that a policeman came up to him, bent over with his hands on his hips, and said, "You again?"

"Oh, I'm not harming anything," Valerie said. "I was here first, after all."

"Yes, you were," the cop said, and wandered away. Later two cops in ordinary clothes took him over into the shade and asked him a lot of questions, obviously about the murder. But they did not seem to care about where Valerie sat. When they were done with him, Valerie went back out and sat down. Pretty soon a girl came up to him.

"Did those policemen bother you?" she asked.

"Oh, no," said Valerie.

The girl went away, and then the next day when Valerie came back to the square shortly after 7:00 A.M., his place had a spilled beer bottle and some vomit in the dirt. Valerie had to spend several minutes cleaning up his little space before he could sit down and get back to work, in what he now thought of as the only comfortable spot in the world.

Zeno, across the street in front of the depot, leaning as usual on the front fender of his maroon Mercedes and sipping a *caffe latte* from a white plastic cup, wondered aloud to his friends if Valerie hadn't perhaps read the works of Carlos Castaneda. "Maybe that's his *spot*," Zeno said.

"That makes complete sense," said Piper, the ex-burglar and knife salesman. "Out of the whole world, that would be the only spot for him. He has a mystical relationship to that spot."

"Probably when he sits on it he covers up the radiation," said Victor sarcastically.

Zeno was amused. "Don't you believe in anything?"

Victor took a Nikon camera from his shoulder bag, made a few quick adjustments, and took a photograph of Valerie. "Sure," he said. "I believe in lots of stuff."

"Name one," said Piper humorously. "Just you name one thing you believe in." He began working his mouth in quick nervous-smile moves. "Just-you-name-one-thing!"

Victor paid no attention to him, putting away his camera after a few shots. He was a good photographer, good enough to make a living at it, if he had needed to make a living.

But Zeno was willing to play. "I believe in. . . let's see . . . money, of course . . ."

"Ah, money! Money will betray you every time! Money is a curse! How can you believe in such a thing?"

Zeno laughed and drained his *latte*. His friend had never had enough money in his life to understand what Zeno meant. Zeno's family were all gifted moneymakers. Zeno himself was considered to be the black sheep of the family because he did not devote every working hour to either making more money or improving his image in the community.

These three had not known the dead woman, although they had seen her at work inside. They were not much affected by her death except as an unusually interesting topic of conversation. Even so, they were able to speak of other things. One thing was the idea for

Zeno and Piper to make a comedy record and clean up. Zeno would ask Piper questions. Piper would pretend that he had been alive for man's entire history, and would offer humorous remarks about contemporary life from that perspective. It was like Mel Brooks' and Carl Reiner's "Two-Thousand-Year-Old Man." In fact, a lot like it.

"In *fact*," said Victor, who was disgusted by the whole thing.

M ILOS lived among the redwoods, two blocks from the depot. The old millsite had been set aside as a park, and by the banks of the stream stood the bare old skeleton of the mill itself. Nearby were a children's playground, with swings, slides, and a big sandbox; a building holding men's and women's toilets, and some very large stumps of the ancient trees that had been cut for timber over a hundred years before. Some of these old stumps were hollow, and in one of these Milos stashed his bedroll during the day and slept at night. The hollow stump was open at the top, with a diameter in places of seven feet, and could be gotten into by scrambling up over the tall sides or through a small almost concealed vent in the side.

The tricky moments were getting in and getting out. Casual visitors to the park, wondering at the cathedral magnificence of the light filtering down through the foliage, might be surprised to see Milos simply pop into existence beside his stump, which was only a few feet from a steep bank of the stream, where it took a wide meander and made a deep clear pool to reflect the light. Or, the ragged figure might be just standing there, his hands behind his back, apparently enjoying the park, and then, as the visitor looks away for a moment, the figure vanishes, leaving not even a chuckle behind.

This did not work with the children who played in the park. The children were infuriating. Milos did not dare come and go in front of them, because they would come up to his hole in the stump, move aside the big hunk of bark he used to conceal it, and poke their little heads in. More than once Milos had found children already inside his hideaway, or signs that children had been and gone. Once he found his bedroll pulled up out of its hidden place, under the ply-wood board Milos had found and then carefully rubbed with vegetation to camouflage. But only once. Usually his home was safe.

And for a few days he hardly left it. There was a lot of bad trouble in town, and Milos hated all the people coming around. For a while he was half-tempted to go back to the city and take up his old place or another, bigger square. But he remembered the city nights, horrible nights of fear. The square here was bad at night, but not like the city.

Finally hunger drove Milos out, bright and early and on another unusually warm morning. The square was empty, but across the street was the strange nigger, just settling himself for the day. This made Milos angry, and halfway across the square he began dancing with rage. This nigger had been the start of it, then somebody got chopped up, that was all Milos knew. He started slapping the bricks with his stick, *whap whap whap,* and shouting, "Gott damn it! Gott damn it!"

"*Haw! Haw! Haw!*" laughed a gigantic black crow, just flapping down onto the bricks about twenty feet from Milos. A big bird, too big to rush at. The crow eyed Milos. "*Haw!*"

"Stinking bird," Milos said. He did not want to back away from this damn bird. But another one flew down with that same harsh laugh, and then in the air more harsh laughter and more black specks that turned into gigantic birds that came and landed on the square. Milos was terrified by the birds. What if they should attack him? He would be helpless. What if he attacked *them?* Waving his stick and screaming, rushing at them . . . but what if they didn't fly away? What if they just laughed at him?

One crow found a crust of bread, threw it up in the air, and caught it in his beak, bite bite, and it was gone.

"I haff to eat, too," Milos said with a hint of apology in his voice, as he backed toward the depot. But he had no money that morning, and there was no one to intimidate. Certainly not the old woman inside. Milos went around the building and over to the seated Valerie.

"Hey, nigger! Wass you doing?"

Valerie ignored the racial slur. "I'm making a bed cover," he said without looking up from his work.

"Das nice," said Milos. He shifted from foot to foot. "Hey, you got any money? I need some coffee."

"Coffee's bad for people," Valerie said. "Besides, I don't give money to people. I don't have any money, anyway."

"Das okay," said Milos gently. He was looking at Valerie's work, nice colors, nice design. "S'beautiful," he said after a while.

"Thank you very much," Valerie said, again without looking up. He just wished the little monster would go away before he flipped out and went crazy or something.

"Hokay," Milos said, and walked around to the square again. A couple of commuters sat in their cars at the side of the square waiting for the depot to open, but Milos did not go over to them. He knew they would not give him anything. He knew both of them by sight. They were both rich fat pigs who deserved to be set fire to in their own cars.

Ha, here come the town drunk. That's what everybody called him, even though at night there were plenty of town drunks to choose from. But this one, Sherman, lived around here in the woods, like Milos. Now look at him. Terrible hangover. Face stunned, under uncombed tangle of brown. Logger clothes, dirty yellow slicker, jeans, boots, shuffling toward the depot back door on the square. *Rap rap rap* on the glass door and then sit down inside the arches on the folding wooden chairs, last vestige of when the buses and before that the trains would pull right up to the building.

Milos watched as the old woman brought out a big hot steaming white plastic cup of coffee for the drunk. Never mind the drunk didn't pay. Never mind the drunk got drunk and yelled at everybody, got in fights, went to jail frequently. The old woman still brought him coffee and stale rolls sometimes. Yes, today, a stale sweet roll, on a paper napkin, right next to the steaming cup of coffee, on the wooden chair next to Sherman.

Milos slowly went over and sat down near the drunk. Sherman grunted something, threw him a slitted glance and went back to the contemplation of his pain. Soon, he took a sip of the coffee, and then put it down again, not noticing that somehow a bite had been removed from his cinnamon roll. He continued to gaze into the middle distance while hearing a nearby slurp. But he paid no attention; the inner view was too compelling.

Thus did Milos and the town drunk break fast together.

THERE were not very many sightseers that day. The depot had lost its fascination as a nearly crime-scene; there were other murders, other sensations, on television and in the newspapers. Tim was glad the fuss had died down for a number of reasons, the most practical of which was that the depot had been losing an unusual number of cups and plates, and an especially large number of the tall glasses they used for the *caffe latte* when it was not ordered to go. People carelessly ordered things for consumption inside the depot, and then seeing the crowded tables, or the warm breezy sunshine outside, would simply take depot dishware out and leave it there. And people took the *latte* glasses home, Tim knew, to use as beer mugs.

So when the white police car squealed to a stop out in front that afternoon Tim was surprised and felt a strong stab of emotion—probably guilt, he thought wearily as he put himself back together. You can quit the Church but the Church never quits you. . .

Tim wiped his hands on his red apron and went out the front door to see what was going on. Fahima, just off for the day, came out and stood beside him, her luxuriant hair loose now, framing the beauty of her face so that Tim had a hard time thinking about anything else. This was a woman, all right. Big, and big across the shoulders, with full warm maternal breasts but a slender waist, slender hips and fine strong long legs. *Ach, Gott,* Tim thought humorously, *Vot a Voman!*

The two young cops by now had Valerie on his feet and one of them had picked up Valerie's bag. Valerie himself clutched his handiwork, his brows dancing, his eyes furious. He towered over the policeman who had him by the arm.

"What do you think you're doing?" he asked rhetorically, for they were herding him into the backseat of the car. Valerie refused to duck his head, as any normal person would do, and the two policemen kept banging his face against the top of the door.

"Help! Help!" Valerie cried, looking Tim right in the eye.

"Oh, God," Tim said helplessly.

"Why are they doing that?" Fahima asked.

"Wait a sec, wait a sec," the little cop said. "We got to spread-search this clown first . . ."

"Oh, yeah," said the other cop, and they half led, half dragged Valerie up to the front fender of their car and bent him over the hood, holding his hands behind him.

"This is police brutality," said Fahima, as if identifying a species of bird.

"Yer doin' it wrong," one cop said to the other. "Cuff him first."

They got out a set of handcuffs and cuffed Valerie's hands behind his back, and then with an embarrassed grin at his partner the short policeman patted Valerie down. Then they wrestled him back and down into the car, the taller cop putting his hand on the back of Valerie's head to make sure he did not bump on the way down. This left Valerie's unfinished bed cover lying on the hood of the police car. Tim and Fahima could hear Valerie bellowing in the car, and then one of the cops got out and grabbed the handiwork and flung it into the back where Valerie sat alone. The police car squealed off around the redwood island and up the street out of sight.

"I wonder what that's all about," Tim said.

"I hope they don't hurt him," Fahima said. "Oh, I missed my bus!"

"He looks pretty Spartan to me," Tim said.

"What is Spartan?"

"Oh, wrong word, I guess. I mean he looks a lot tougher than he looks. Ha ha."

"But what is Spartan?"

"From Sparta. Ancient Greece."

"Oh, yes. But why does it mean tough?"

"Don't you know the story of the little Spartan boy? Every American is raised on this story."

She had not heard it. She looked up into his plain honest face and smiled happily. She liked Tim. He was such a nice man.

"Well, these Spartan boys lived like soldiers, and they weren't supposed to have any pets. But this one kid found a baby fox, and kept it hidden. One morning the boys are called outside, and the boy hides his fox under his tunic. You know *tunic*? Okay, so the little fox starts to bite and scratch the boy's stomach, but the little boy doesn't cry out! He makes no sound, he is brave. He becomes a hero for not crying out in pain." Tim wondered if she understood, because she had a puzzled look on her face, and then a determined frown.

"What are you thinking?" he asked.

"Little boy should have said, 'We have *right* to have foxes!'"

This answer dumbfounded Tim. He had never thought of such a thing. Tim walked around the building with her, and then on impulse, across the square to where the bus stopped. They talked about matters of the day, but Tim, who wanted to stay and talk, finally had to say, "Well, I have to get back."

"See you in the morning," she said. Tim wanted to kiss her goodbye. What a stupid thought. She was herself probably thinking about sore feet and home, playing with her cat, making dinner for her husband. Deflated, Tim trudged back to the depot and the utterly fascinating tasks of Modern Management.

He had forgotten all about Valerie.

WHEN Valerie came back, four mornings later, he found that someone had dug up the ground where he was accustomed to sit, all the way from the fading red curbstone to the decorative volcanic rocks that held the plaque which Valerie had never read. The old dirt had been replaced with rich black new dirt, and into it had been transplanted several flowering plants. Primroses. Very pretty with all their colors, and glistening with wet from the watering of the night before.

Valerie at once busied himself with retransplanting the primroses, closer to one another and well back from the curb, although curving nicely so that Valerie's spot was surrounded by plants. The fresh potting soil was still wet on Valerie's spot, so he got several double handfuls of gravel from across in front of the depot. Once the old woman came out to feed the sparrows who lived in the tree outside the kitchen window.

"They've been busy over there while I was gone," Valerie said. "I think the city fathers would like to see me vanish."

"Maybe so," Dorothy said. She watched the little birds fly down and begin pecking at the dried crusts she had dropped for them. Always the same, first the one little bird, then that one, then that one . . . she knew all the sparrows by their markings. She liked English sparrows, even though everybody told her they were pests. They were there winter and summer, not flying off to Mexico like some, when the weather got cold. It never really got cold here, though. Not like Back East. Dorothy was a refugee from Back East and its weather. The only drawback out here was the earthquakes.

A black panel truck pulled up and a man got out with a bundle of newspapers for the depot. He waved at Valerie, who was just crossing the street with his last double handful of gravel, and thus did the press first take notice of him.

Valerie was soon crosslegged and comfortable, the work across his knees, the needles clicking. And soon after that the sun broke through the trees beneath the square and struck Valerie on the forehead, sending deep yellow waves of comforting heat into his brain. His brain needed the calming. Valerie had been in jail. There had been violent arguments about his things, which he wished to keep with him, and which the police wished to store someplace. The police won, of course, and Valerie was stripped against his will, dressed in an orange jumpsuit that stank of laundry chemicals and thrown into the felony tank with a lot of horrible people.

Meditation helped, and Valerie could sit crosslegged facing the wall during the days and it was all right. If he had been allowed to have his work, he might have been perfectly content; after all, the bunk was no worse than the one he regularly slept on. Although the blanket left something to be desired. The real problems came at night, when somebody would unscrew the light or something and plunge the place into almost total darkness. Then all sorts of horrible nastiness would take place, things Valerie would rather not dwell on, the usual disgusting episodes.

Then they stuck him in a cell by himself and the turnkey said, "Sorry about that, you should have spoke up," but Valerie wasn't speaking to him. He just sat there and meditated until they finally let him out. They told him he had not been in jail at all, although he wondered how that could be, and they let him out and kindly suggested he go home and mind his own business.

His old ex-marine mentor was out there looking mad as hell. He must have been called to come up there and get him. "I'm sorry they troubled you," Valerie said to him as they left the building.

"Git in the car," the old jocker said. The charges had been

dropped. What charges? Well, maybe there never had been any charges. "The cops do what they want," said the ex-marine. "You got to keep outta their way."

"They can just keep out of *my* way," Valerie said.

The sun was burning sweetly on his head now, the morning moving around him easily, the work going well, his mind relaxed and flabby and pleasant. The girl who came up to him was nice, innocent-looking, concerned. A nice person, leaning forward, her hands on her knees. She asked him a lot of questions about his work, his life, and what the police had done to him. He tried to answer her questions without getting personal. He did not like to reveal personal information about himself or his past. What was past was past. She was a reporter, and took down what he said on a little pad of paper. She had a young man with her with a black beard and a lot of cameras. The young man took several pictures, and in one picture Valerie was asked to stand up, holding his work in front of himself so people could see how it was coming.

"Will that be in color?"

"I'm afraid not," the young man said.

"That's too bad," Valerie said, seating himself once again.

"What's going on?"

The police were here again, always noisy, dusty, the car doors open. Valerie sighed, readying himself for a struggle. But the girl started talking to the police, holding up her notebook, and the police lost their tempers and went away. That was fine. Valerie got in a good day's work.

The next morning, when the black van parked in front of the depot and the man got out with his bundles of newspapers, he grinned and yelled over at Valerie: "Hey, yer a star!"

The photograph appeared on page 34, in the People section. It showed Valerie seated, intent on his work. With his nearly shaved head, dramatic eyebrows, and hairline mustache he looked a little sinister to some, but the caption overhead said, CURBSTONE GURU, and the article below, using innuendo, suggestion, and other tricks of the trade, hinted that the local police were harassing Valerie because they were being frustrated in the Slain Singer case.

Words of Valerie's, taken out of context, gave the article its philosophical base.

Later that morning Victor read a couple of quotes to his friends Piper and Zeno. "I think everybody should have a place," was one. "The police should have better things to do," was another. Victor looked up from his paper, his eyes merry, his mouth in its nest of black beard round with tart amusement.

"Words to live by, huh, fellas?"

"Very profound," Piper said. He looked a little puzzled, and worked his smile mechanism more than usual as he rapidly smoked a cigarette. "I don't get it. What's so profound about that guy?"

Zeno explained to Victor, "He's a little hurt the press didn't write *him* up."

"That's it," said Piper. "Good evening, ladies and germs, ha ha, a funny thing happened to me on the way to the depot." He spoke rapidly, looking around at his imaginary audience. "Police jokes," he said. "I don't know any police jokes."

"Maybe the police just aren't funny," Zeno said.

Victor was on his way across the street with his newspaper. "Have you seen this yet?" he asked Valerie. Valerie looked up, squinted in the sunlight and said, "No, I haven't."

"You want to read it?"

"No, thank you."

"I can read it to you," Victor said.

"Well, I can read, if that's what you mean, but go ahead if you want to."

Victor read him the article tonelessly and then bent down, holding out the paper. "See the picture?" he asked.

Valerie peered at the photograph of himself critically. "That's not a very good photograph, is it?"

"No," admitted Victor, who could have taken a better one standing on his left ear.

"Thank you for reading it to me. I'm so embarrassed. I didn't mean to say all those things."

"I wouldn't worry about it," Victor said, and went back to his friends. Others were drifting out of the depot or down the street to look at Valerie. Here and there a camera clicked as people attempted to duplicate the newspaper photograph for themselves. The first time a police car came through the area it had to move slowly, because people were standing in the street. The police car did not stop. From various directions came boos and hisses, but as one officer remarked to the other, they did not seem to be hostile boos and hisses. "More like humorous. We're the goat today," is how he put it. "Nothing to get hot about." They most pointedly did not stop in front of Valerie. The word was out. "Leave that crazy bitch alone," the force had been told, "until the shit stops hitting the fan."

This did not suit the officers at all, but what could they do? The world was full of things they could not fix or change. Valerie was just one more of them, right now. "Don't throw her in jail, the crazy bitch loves it!" was one comment, and there was a rumor among the officers that Valerie had made eighteen hundred dollars in his time in jail, a record.

The day got hotter and hotter, a real California early summer heat wave beginning. The flies inside the depot multiplied until there seemed to be several for each table. By two in the afternoon all the *latte* glasses had been stolen and the square was thick with people. Many of them commented that it was just like a carnival out there, with this crazy black man (or whatever he was!) defying the police. And everybody seemed to know that the police had been warned to leave Valerie alone, and this increased the carnival feeling. It was, "Heigh ho, the lunatics are in charge!"

Milos was even being courted. There were so many people crowding around Valerie to congratulate him, ask his advice, look at his bed cover, or just gaze at him with curiosity and admiration, that people who couldn't get close enough to Valerie would talk to anybody who looked even slightly crazy.

Milos responded to this by being alternately canny and crazy. For example, here came a fat white rat of a man, in plump tennis clothes, shoes so white they blinded, thick hard legs with thick nasty-looking powerful blood vessels, ropy red neck, blank face, thick ears. "Is this the village square?" was his first stupid question. Milos responded by frowning thoughtfully and stroking his chin whiskers. "Yes," he said finally, after deep thought.

"Yeah," the white rat said. "Where's that guy? Over there?"

"What guy?"

"You know, from the paper?"

"I am dat one!" Milos said dramatically. "Dis time you da crazy man! I'm da guy! Craphunter! Damn white rat!"

The guy fled and Milos danced. Several people watched him. Some pointed, some grinned. He danced some more.

Sherman, the town drunk, took heavy advantage of the crowd, hitting on all these commuter types in their weekend jogging outfits. In half an hour he had made over twenty dollars. His line that day was taken as funny by most of the people he hit on; some were frightened by it; nearly all contributed when he said, lugubriously, his reddened eyes looking right into the mark's: "Hey, Mister, I need a dime to call my parole officer."

Soon Sherman was drunk, and not on wine, either. Good dark Rainier Ale, followed by a pint of Jack Daniels whiskey. Slowly but surely he went from cheerful to baleful, and by sundown he was as fiercely drunk as he had ever been. The cops weren't around to bother him, and that was just fine. He wanted to talk to that dumb fuckin' nigger anyway, about all this shit. What the fuck was going on, was what he wanted to know. He made his way around the depot, giving the place a wide berth because by this time of day it was full of scumbags and besides Sherman was eighty-six and had been. But the place where the nigger sat was empty.

"Smart nigger," Sherman mumbled to himself. He turned back toward the square, looking, a little early, for something to fight.

THE next day brought two television crews to the square. By coincidence they both arrived at the same time, about ten in the morning, when it was just getting hot. There were not many local people around, but the two crews knew from experience that they would themselves draw a crowd before long. And they wanted a crowd. That was the story. The two on-camera people knew each other only by sight, but greeted one another with affectionate hugs and smiles that seemed to say, "Long time no see, old friend!"

The male, a sleekly handsome darkeyed man who made over eighty thousand dollars a year, and who was getting a little thick below camera, invited the female, who was younger, pretty, and very serious, over to the depot for a cup of coffee. He knew she didn't make anything like as much money as he did, and he was gracious to the point of offering to buy the lady a croissant ("Hey, these look pretty good!"), but she put him on his guard at once by saying, "No, thanks, I have to watch my weight!" and then thoroughly upset him when they sat by the big windows looking out over the square, and, as she wiped up invisible crumbs from the tabletop, asked him why he of all people had been given such a Mickey Mouse assignment.

"Mickey Mouse?" he said with a stab of fear. What did she know?

With her thumb she indicated Valerie, out front, who had been seated crosslegged at work for hours. "The coo-coo," she said. "It's not exactly the visit of the Queen. I'm used to it, heck, my next story is in Livermore. But you. I thought you just sat there in the studio and sent others to cover these major newsbreaks."

"Ha ha," he said by way of explanation. She must have known, then. His star was setting. Everybody in the business knew it, everybody below him was after his job. Even this woman. Well, why not? Women have been taking all the other jobs, why not his?

Outside the window, Milos danced for them, not knowing who they were. They paid no attention to him. Looking at the glass they could faintly see their own reflections, and that was enough.

"Well, let's go make a slow newsday even slower," the male said finally, getting up and waiting politely. As she stood, the woman got almost too close to him, coming up right under his chin and turning her eyes up at him with an amused little crinkle, and he could smell her perfume. He grinned automatically. They left the depot without busing their dishes. Tim cleaned up after them. He liked the woman on the air, but thought the man pompous.

They were too late to interview many of the morning regulars. But Piper was still around, smoking nervously and watching. Then suddenly he found himself staring into a shoulder camera while a grinning woman thrust a microphone at him.

This was, for Piper, the opportunity of a lifetime.

It was also a terrible crisis. He had always known that when this moment came, he would be brilliant, he would be killingly funny, he would be sophisticated, suave, and the world would quickly take him from this unnatural obscurity and . . .

But. Here was this little woman with her goddamn microphone. "I know your face," Piper said to her. He made several quick nervous smile moves. He wanted a cigarette. His feet had gone cold and actually hurt.

"Never mind that," she said. The interview was brief, and Piper could tell from her expression that she was disappointed in him. He was disappointed, too. His wit had deserted him. He had said nothing funny, nothing informative.

But that night in his little basement studio he lay cool in his bed and watched his tiny television set, and was not disappointed.

There, in the midst of the others, was Piper himself, looking a little strange, saying, "I don't understand what's goin' on." Then they cut to this starry-eyed woman who said Valerie was inspiring her.

Piper slept fitfully. He wondered if any of his friends had seen him on television. He wondered what would happen the next day. He knew the media could have a powerful effect on events. The media had the power to create or destroy. This he knew. He wondered if it had created or destroyed him. Ha. There had been one moment of satisfaction—when he had sold that camera guy a set of cookware.

But the next morning neither Victor nor Zeno asked him about his appearance, joked with him about it, or even acknowledged that it had happened. And Piper was damned if he would bring it up. Besides, there was too much going on. Today the square and the street were really jammed with people, all apparently to see Valerie. Once again the cops had to set up traffic controls and there was a festival atmosphere.

Victor kept busy taking photographs, and Zeno was quiet, leaning as usual against the front fender of his maroon Mercedes sedan, sipping his *latte* and watching the crowd.

Piper said, "Where will it all end? The cover of *Time?* 'Sixty Minutes?' The United Nations?"

"I think it will end right here," Victor said. He took one last picture of Valerie, who was nearly surrounded by admirers, including a couple of pretty women.

Then a young man came up to them and stood with his hands behind his back, joining them without being invited. After a couple of uncomfortable moments, the young man said brightly, "He's really inspiring, isn't he?"

"Yeah," said Victor, coldly.

"I mean, people talk about doing stuff, but he just does it. He's free!"

"That's not what I heard," said Victor tartly.

When the young man went into the depot he stood in line in front of the high glassed-in counter smiling at anybody whose eye he could catch. He wore a white dress shirt open at the collar, clean blue jeans, and uncomfortable-looking brown shoes, unpolished and rundown at the heels enough to give him a peculiar bowlegged gait when he walked. Fahima was in the slot taking orders, a strand of her long dark hair loose on her forehead. The young man smiled at her.

"The coffee should be free," he said. "Everything should be free."

"Forty cents," Fahima said tiredly. The young man was still smiling at her, and so she gave him a tired smile. Her shift was about to end. That was nice. Fahima was glad her job was menial, even glad that it paid so badly. But ah! Was she glad when her shift ended! This terrible job was good experience for when she got back home and would work in a factory with people who had never had anything but factory worker lives. She would try to help them, to give them hope, and, of course, to make them revolutionaries. Without hope, without plans, without a different future, menial labor could be horrible, forever to wash one dish, turn one piece, to endlessly hack at the endless face of the eternal coal mine . . .

The young man in the white shirt stood with his steaming mug of coffee, looking around the room for a place to sit. The depot was more crowded than usual, thanks to the television of the night before, and so the young man had to finally sit at a chair at the large round table in the middle of the room, where three other people already sat, busy in conversation, two men and a woman. They looked at the young man, and then went back to their private conversation. The young man sat in the pleasant buzz of talk and laughter, looking around him at the assembled humanity, and his heart went out to them all.

"It is wonderful to be alive," he said pretty loudly, but no one responded. The buzz just went on.

His name was Theo and he had cut summer school that morning miles away and hitchhiked to see Valerie. On the television the night before, Valerie had said that everybody ought to have a place, that there ought to be a place for everybody. Theo felt that he did not yet have a place. He was not liked at school, by either the other students or the teachers. And his parents had no use for him. He seemed to embarrass them. His older brother did not much like him, either. His brother was an athlete, a good student. His father was an engineer. His mother played cards. They had their lives all worked out.

Theo, on the other hand, could not concentrate well enough to get good grades. He had no physical skills and was not handsome or anything, just another hunk of human waste. Faceless. Placeless. But. He had over sixty bucks in his pocket. With a thrill he thought that maybe he just would not go home that night. That he would run away now, and never go home again. Go out and find his place. Because there had to be a *place* for him. He took two of the little blue pills the doctor had given him to calm him down. The coffee was getting cold. Soon it would be time to cross the street and speak to Valerie. He did not know what to expect, or even that Valerie's name was Valerie.

Tim was at his own little table working on his order list. He saw the kid in the white shirt sitting there looking around openly eavesdropping on people. Tim also noticed the slightly feverish look in the kid's eye, and marked him down as a potential troublemaker. Among others. Among others. Because it was not just this one kid. There were a lot of people attracted by the media blitz who were not just rubberneckers, sightseers, curiosity hounds. There was, indeed, a surplus of crazy-looking types. The kid had the look—too much expression on the face, too eager to join the conversation of others. Tim shrugged to himself. It was really none of his business unless the kid acted up here in the depot.

Right then the young man in the white shirt got up, smiling at no one, everyone, leaving his mug behind. Apparently no one read the signs posted everywhere to bus your own dishes. With all these strangers, a lot of crap was being left on tables. The kid went outside and Tim promptly forgot about him. He had problems of his own. Not the ordering, that was routine, almost a pleasure, since in ordering, Tim knew exactly what he was doing. A certainty that seemed to avoid him in the rest of his life. His chief worry now, at this minute, was that he might be too interested in Fahima. She was a married woman and he was a married man. And besides, she was about to leave the country for good, go home to Iran, and probably get shot dead or thrown into prison. Maybe tortured. Tim winced. The big problem had been last night, at home. At the hour of let-down, as Tim called it, he had his usual two drinks with his wife, and did his usual day's debriefing, just kind of maundering on about the events of the day until the liquor took control and allowed him to relax into his evening. But after a while his wife had said, "You've got Fahima on the brain, don't you?" And Tim realized that he had been talking about her nonstop for about half an hour. Fahima this, Fahima that.

"You'd think she was the best employee you ever had," Claire said. Tim looked over at her, comfortable deep in her favorite chair with its bridge lamp, her face just in the shadows, her drink tinkling in her lap. Tim felt once again a sadness for Claire, a sadness that always led to his feeling bad. She was tall and dark, like Fahima, yes, the genotype of his dreams . . . except, except his wife was twelve years older, and was beginning to lose the war against her own flesh. She had simply not snapped back from her last pregnancy, he thought, and then castigated himself for thinking it. That had all been long before they had gotten married. She had been overweight around the middle, in the ass and upper thighs, when they had met, while Tim was still in the hell of watching the restaurant he had so carefully built into *something* be turned inexorably into a dump by the partner his ex-wife's father had wished on him, a man whose first idea of good management was to buy less expensive meats, which quickly got rid of all the regular customers who had good taste. Anyway, she had come in with a couple of old regulars and Tim had sat with them, flirting with Claire before he had ever seen her from the midriff down.

Well, one thing led to another, didn't it? What could one say to that? They dated, she was bright, sexy, and carried herself well, in spite of the extra weight. *Hey! Let's face facts! You have a wee roll around the breadbasket yourself!* Yeah, okay. But why did he marry her and assume command of a brand new family, complete with children?

Tim finished the last of his second drink, eyeing his wife over the rim of the glass. The truth was, he had married her because he had thought he loved her. To him that feeling of tenderness, of protectiveness, of comfort and happiness, had been love. And now, God damn it, admit it to yourself sitting here in front of a blank television set while the kids thump around upstairs and Claire sits fatly looking at nothing, admit it, when you came to work at the depot early on the mornings when she worked, seeing her—no, just driving down the freeway—no, back, sitting alone at the breakfast table over his morning coffee, his heart would leap at the thought of seeing her. And when he *did* see her! And there would be delight in *her* eyes. Was it because of him! Or was she like that with everybody?

Tim did not know. He looked up and over through the glass of the display, to where Fahima stood bent over the salad board, working. She looked up, just then, and met his eyes. Modestly she dropped her eyes. But she smiled, too. For Tim. Tim, oh, Tim. Such a *fine* man!

THE kid in the white shirt did not actually get to talk to Valerie personally. There was a group around the seated man, and Theo joined it, just as Valerie was saying, "Yes, I think every little town and city should just take little spare places like this one and turn them over to the people, bits of parking strip, little corners of front yards, put in flowers and let people have these places when they don't have anyplace else to go."

"Would you want some squatter in your front yard?" asked a skeptic, and Valerie's needles clicked furiously. Valerie did not choose to answer, so somebody else said, "Property is a burden if you don't share it."

After a while Theo drifted away, a little disappointed. He had hoped for something more . . . thrilling. He went into the depot and had another cup of coffee, but it made him feel nervous and a little giddy. He went out onto the square, where there were people sunning themselves, standing around talking, sitting in the shade against the wall or in the alcove behind the arches. Theo found a place to sit against the wall, hunkered down into it, and began to think about his own future. If he was going to be home in time for dinner he had better start pretty soon. He could take a bus to the city and then another one to his home. But if he missed dinner, no one would miss him. He would come in late and either get yelled at or everybody would be asleep. Or, he had sixty dollars. He could take a room someplace and stay around here, see what was going on. There were some interesting-looking people around here.

But by twilight, he was pretty lonely. No one had been very polite to him when he spoke to them, and the kids his own age who came and went had ignored him. Now there was a group of men, mostly dressed in pieces of uniform, sitting around the concrete sides of a raised flower bed. Some of the men had bottles in brown paper bags. That was an idea, too. He went over toward them, a little hesitantly, but as he approached, a guy in a dirty yellow slicker grinned up at him and said, "Hey, kid, you got three bucks I can borrow? I need some pepperoni sticks."

That got a general laugh. Theo dug in his pocket automatically and came up with a few bills. He gave three dollars to the man, who thanked him and headed off for the liquor store. Theo sat down a little way from the group and was quiet. After a while, the men started talking among themselves again, and the one who had borrowed the three dollars came back with two bottles of ale in a brown paper bag. "Green death," he said, uncapped one of the bottles expertly on the edge of the concrete and took down about half of it.

"Sherman, you're a fuggin' drunkard," somebody said.

Sherman laughed, and took down some more green death. "What I need now is a cig-ret," he said. He leaned forward to peer over at the kid in the white shirt. He frowned at the kid, a mock frown. "You got any cig-rets, kid? What the fuck do you mean, comin' round here without no cig-rets?"

"I can get some," Theo said, with a twinge of anxiety at being exploited, but Sherman the drunk said, "Naw, hell," and pulled a single long filtertipped cigarette from under his clothing somewhere. "Had one all the time."

"God," said one guy in khaki watchcap, dirty camouflage fatigue pants and a dirty old tee shirt proclaiming: EXPECT NOTHING: "I remember those damned machine-rolled marijuana cigarettes. Opium soaked."

"Ten bucks a pack of twenty," said another man dreamily. He

picked at his horny dirty bare feet as he talked, and sipped from a half pint in a brown paper bag. "Smoke a couple of those and head out a'wastin'."

"Dinky dao," said another dreamily.

"I'll dinky yer fuckin' dao," Sherman said. "But I sure wish I had some of that goddam opium right about now. I get bad dreams, men. I need help."

"Is there somewhere we could get some?" the kid in the white shirt asked. The men gave each other significant looks, and Sherman put it into words: "You got the money?"

Theo realized he had made a mistake, but what was money good for, after all? It just got you into trouble. "Sure, I got the money," he said. The others looked at him, more friendly now.

Theo said, "Is there some of that stuff around? Can I buy some of those soaked cigarettes?"

Everybody laughed. Sherman was kind: "Kid, that shit's long ago and far away. Sure, there's drugs around, but it ain't like the old days. An' it never will be again."

"You can Amen that shit," somebody said, and there were grunts of approval.

"Here comes Nifty Nick," somebody said. The little man who silently joined them was dressed the same—old uniform parts, too many of them, beard, strange little haunted animal eyes. He just stood there in front of the group, sort of swaying. Sherman offered him a drink of ale, which he took, and passed the bottle back. Theo had not seen any other bottles passed, yet another of the men also gave his bottle to Nifty Nick. They seemed to treat him with deference, and after only a few minutes Theo could see that the little man was truly mad, as if fear had long ago taken his sanity, and replaced it with nothing.

Nervously Theo jumped to his feet. "Here, sit here," he said to

Nifty Nick, but the little man just looked at him with scared eyes and said nothing.

"See you guys later," Theo said, and began to walk down to the bus stop.

"Hey, what about the money?" somebody yelled.

Theo learned with a shock that to spend even one night in a motel room would cost him most of the money he had. He was hot and tired from walking almost two miles to find the motel, and if there had been a bus in front of him he would have gotten on it and gone somewhere, probably home. But there was no bus. Slowly he walked back to the town square. It was full dark now.

There were some light standards around the square, with old-fashioned street lamps throwing down circles of light in the gloom. Lights came also from the depot. Theo could see shadowy figures here and there. He put aside the problem of where he was going to sleep that night. He felt excited, not the least bit hungry, expectant, as if something important were about to happen to him.

"Hey, Skank," somebody said to him. He turned and saw three boys about his own age, hard-looking kids with short haircuts. The one talking to him smiled. "Who the fuck are you?"

"I'm Theo," he said. He felt fear. He knew guys like this at home and stayed the hell away from them. All three seemed cold and ruthless.

"What the fuck is a Theo?" one of them said. Theo was surrounded now. "What the fuck you doin' around here? Nobody ever seen you before."

"I was just," he said, but the leader grabbed his shoulder and said roughly, "Give us the fuckin' money, Skank."

Theo knew better than to try philosophy on these punks. He had a trick: since losing his wallet a couple of years ago Theo had taken to putting his bills, folded once, in his front pocket and keeping his wallet with its ID and other personal stuff in his hip pocket. Now he reached for his hip, saying, "I ain't got no money," and handing the wallet to the lead guy.

The guy didn't even look inside, but threw the wallet away, as far as he could, sailing over the parked cars along the side of the square and into the weeds of the little corporation yard.

"Hey, my wallet!" Theo cried, and started to run after it, but one of the boys tripped him and he landed on his hands, just barely saving his face from the bricks. His hands stung and inside he was really frightened. But as he got up and started moving, the three boys did not come after him. He went down to the gate of the yard, which was closed, but he could easily have gotten over it. The yard was dark now, just one naked light bulb over in a corner. He would not be able to find anything tonight.

Back outside the depot he saw a familiar face, the man he had given three dollars to earlier. "Oh, hi," he said to the man in the yellow slicker. The man looked at him stupid drunk, his lips wet, his eyes like stones. Theo went past him and into the depot. It seemed suddenly like a safe haven, after the outside. He gratefully ordered a mug of coffee and sat by himself with his coffee, trying to think. He was a million miles from home. Why?

He did not know why. He only knew that he felt excited again. He *knew* something was going to happen to him.

He had come to see the guru. Now the guru was gone, and hadn't been much anyway. There was really nothing to do but go home, another of his stupid ideas gone bad. He had another mug of coffee, and then another one. He listened to a couple of conversations around him, but did not hear anything important, or even interesting. Just the usual blah-blah. He had to go to the bathroom, and, just like him, he sat there so long having to pee he could hardly get up and cross over to the restroom door, and when he did there was somebody in there, and then the woman said, "We're closing," and he said, "But I have to use the bathroom," and she said, "Why'n't you go outside?" and winked at him, and so he went outside and heard her snap the lock behind him. Aced out again. And in pain.

He walked over through the chevroned empty parking lot with its forest of meters toward the corporation yard fence, with its weeds growing tall along the outside of the fence as well as thickly in the yard. He would pee against the fence. As he made his way toward the fence he heard a distant whooping behind him and then a short burst of angry siren. As he tried to pee he heard yelling and then it stopped. The pee would not come, and he cursed himself for waiting too long. Now he would have to squat somewhere. God damn it.

"Hey, said a voice behind him. He turned. It was one of the old vets, from before. "Oh, hi," he said. He could hardly see the man's face. The man stood close to him, his voice throaty, his breath hot and rich with booze. "I found some dope if you still got the money."

"Dope?" Theo vaguely remembered they talked about opium-laced marijuana. That would be something. Get really high and ride home, the long way home, on a bus all high and mighty. He followed the man.

They trudged up the darkened street a couple of blocks, silently, and Theo began to wonder where they were going, when the houses and shops gave way to the redwoods that hung dark over everything. Now they entered the woods. Obviously, some kind of park.

"Where we goin'?" he asked.

"Shh," the guy said.

The ground was springy and silent under his feet. They went down a slope between trees, and then suddenly Theo found himself surrounded. A match struck, and faces lit up—only four of them, all bums, beards, caps, eyes.

"You got the money?" came a harsh whisper.

"Uh, how much?"

"God love you, brother, forty bucks will guarangoddamtee yuh high fer a week!"

"Uh, could I get twenty dollars worth?"

"What the fuck is this? Some kinda rip-off? Forty bucks!"

He got out the money and felt it taken, something small put into his hand, his hand closed around it by the dirty horny fingers of the guy who took his money.

"What did you give me?"

But the men were laughing and talking now, in low voices, passing around a bottle.

"Here, kid, have a drink," one of them said, and Theo felt the raw whiskey in his throat. The something in his hand felt like a piece of paper. That was it, he had heard of LSD-soaked blotting paper. He put the paper in his mouth. Dry. He swallowed and it would not go down. He held out his hand for the whiskey pint and took a quick sip, swallowing hotly, almost gagging, but the paper went down.

"Ah," he said.

"Hey, wud you do?"

"Huh? I took the stuff. Swallowed it."

"Jesus Christ."

"What's wrong?"

"That was eight hits of acid you took."

"Is that too much?"

"Oh, what an asshole," somebody said.

Theo stumbled around in the redwood park for a while and then finally found the sidewalk. He made his way down the street. He did not feel anything except a burning in his throat from the booze. He hoped the buses ran that late. He wanted to go home.

Victor, Zeno, and Piper had not been meeting in the mornings with all that much regularity, but now it became a ritual. Piper was the only one of the three who hung out around the square all day and sometimes even early in the evenings, and so the others might start the morning quizzing Piper about the events of the day before.

Piper himself began each day the same. Although he did not drink he acted brooding and darkly pained as he sipped his hot black coffee and smoked cigarettes out in the sunshine. Thus, at first, he was not expected to be funny. He could react with grunts and rolling eyes to any jokes offered to him. The other two guys liked to put him on a little, but it did not bother him. He knew, as they knew, that they were several cuts above Piper on any socioeconomic ladder, and so they were entitled to score off him. But the little worm always turned, didn't it? Ha ha.

The maroon Mercedes came up the street, curved carefully around Valerie and turned at last into the parking space right in front of the depot, where Piper leaned against the parking meter holding his plastic cup in one hand and his cigarette in the other. The two men only grunted at one another as Zeno went past into the place for his *latte*. While Zeno was inside, Victor came walking around the corner slowly, as if in pain. Victor always parked his car, a spotless old Malibu, some distance away. Victor never bought coffee or anything else inside the depot, unless he was overcome by an attack of appetite. He could do nothing about these attacks except eat. Should an attack strike him he might eat at one standing (he would not even bother to sit) five or six bagel dogs with relish and mustard, half a dozen sweet rolls, and a couple of slices of pie.

Today, however, he was on one of his diets. After a few minutes of standing quietly next to Piper, Victor removed a carrot from his shoulder bag and began to eat.

"Daah, what's up, Doc?" Piper said.

After Zeno came back out, and a few peaceful moments had passed, Piper said, "Wow, wait til you see the new ones."

"New whats?" asked Zeno.

"The new inhabitants," Piper said. "The new crazies." He sucked on his teeth, took a puff from his cigarette and looked off. "The Queen of the Nile and her consort."

Victor snorted. "I saw them yesterday," he said.

Piper looked hurt. "You were here yesterday afternoon? Where was I? Oh, yeah, out sellin'."

"The Queen of the Nile?" Zeno asked.

"Apparently this woman is several thousand years old," Victor said with a straight face. It had become their style to talk about the crazies as if their stories were true. "She has pictures to prove it."

"Yeah," said Piper. "She wears pictures on her dress, cut out of magazines, newspapers, I don't know where she gets them all."

"But inconspicuous," Victor said seriously. "Her consort, the King, usually explains her story."

"Did you talk to them?" Zeno asked.

"I heard 'em talk."

Not long afterward, just as Zeno was about to leave, a dirty old white Chevy pulled up next to his car. The car looked lived-in, and it was. The man behind the wheel was longhaired and bearded, with calculating eyes in a cruel wolfish face. The woman sitting next to him seemed small and mousey, and when they got out that impression continued. The pictures pinned all over her clothing *were* oddly inconspicuous, her dress old and tattered, a floor-length gown that had dragged in the dirt too long. In spite of the heat she wore a couple of cardigan sweaters and a jacket. Her hair was brown and mousey, her face pinched and small. The King towered over her, but did not help her get out. He walked ahead of her into the depot with a nod at the three watchers. She smiled at them faintly, shyly, as she passed in his wake.

"That's them?" Zeno asked. "Don't look like much to me."

"They were summoned here by Valerie's presence," Victor said with a straight face. "The King will explain Valerie to you if you like."

"I get it," said Zeno.

"The Queen is the one," said Piper. "She goes up to people and asks them in this polite little voice if they would like to go to Karnak or Memphis, although I don't know why anybody would want to go to Memphis."

"Ha ha," said Victor. "Memphis, Egypt, of course."

"There's writing all over her pictures, too. At least it looks like writing."

"I'll tell you what *I* think," Zeno said. "I think Valerie got his message out on the television, so now every nut in range wants to get *his* message out on the television. Thus the nut parade."

"You better listen to the King," Victor said seriously. "He might have a message for you."

"She gets payments," Piper said. "And she gets some kind of medication to keep her from flipping. But he takes her money and he takes her drugs. He's a leech."

"The word is consort," Victor said with a straight face.

"Well, I have to get to my guru," Zeno said, also with a straight face.

"Your guru," Victor said.

"At least my guru is deep into the fiscal system," said Zeno with a grin.

WHEN the Queen of the Nile and her consort came into the depot Tim felt an immediate dislike for him and pity for her. The man bought and paid for two small coffees with an assortment of coins while the woman arranged herself at a table by the big arched windows and then smiled blankly, sweetly, at nothing. Others watched her covertly. She looked half gypsy, half waif, thought Tim. He wished Fahima had been working that morning, but no, she was home probably lying in bed with hand-some Hassan, eagerly talking politics in Farsi. Tim tried to imagine her naked, but something in his mind prevented the images from coming in clear. He had no trouble imagining other girls naked. But Fahima, even in his mind, seemed to laugh and say, "Oh, no, Teem, this is wrong." Teem, Teem. He loved the way she said his name.

With an effort, Tim took his mind off Fahima. There were two other employees here working right now, Monika from Germany, stocky smart little blonde who simply never stopped working except on her breaks when she would dash outside for a cigarette; and Greg, the high school boy who worked here for low wages even though his parents lived up among the redwoods in a splendid though some-what gloomy multilevel home. Greg's ambitions were manifold and diffuse, as he himself put it, and he was a good worker unless the pretty girls came in and flirted with him. Then he would redden and make jokes and spill the soup. Tim liked him.

Tim saw the Queen get up and go over to some people sitting at the big round table in the middle. He started to come around the counter, to tell her not to do that, and then stopped himself. She looked pretty harmless, and was smiling at the people while she spoke. She had a piece of paper in her hand, and she put it down on the table and wrote something on it. Then she went back to her own table, and the people at the round table laughed among themselves.

Later, Tim was at the little table by the double back doors trying to work on ordering supplies and debating whether to change laundries when the Queen (by now he as well as everybody else had heard their nicknames) approached him shyly with her piece of paper. He sat up stiffly, in a pose of guarded rejection. She put the piece of paper in front of him. It was a color reproduction of a photograph of some great ancient Egyptian statues, rising out of the Nile. The picture had obviously been torn from a magazine.

"Would you like to visit this place?" She asked Tim in a quiet little voice. Tim could see writing all across the picture—but no. It was not writing. It just *looked* like writing.

He had noticed, when she first came in, that she was a homely, mousey woman of indiscriminate age—perhaps thirty-five, or forty—but now as she smiled down at Tim he thought to himself, amazed, that she was strangely beautiful. He felt a powerful attraction for her.

"Uh, no, thank you," he said.

"I could write your name down, and then you could go," she said. She had her little ballpoint pen ready.

"Oh, no, thank you," he said. "I'm really too busy."

"Yes, you're the manager," she said, and for some reason it surprised Tim that she knew this. She went back to her table and Tim saw her consort's slitted eyes ruthlessly gaze at him.

Don't look at me like that, you bastard, Tim thought. He really did not like the look of the man. Cruelty and coldness ruled his harshly handsome face. His hair and beard were grizzled, and Tim could see at his open throat curly white hairs on his chest. Mister Macho, Tim thought unkindly. He hoped they would go away soon.

But they did not. After an hour in the depot they moved outside to the square, where they soon gathered a crowd. Tim could see them through the windows, seated side by side on one of the raised concrete flower beds. There were a couple of local types standing around, and a kid in a white shirt sitting at their feet, hugging his knees and listening to the consort talk.

Late that day, after a lot of paperwork, interviews with potential employees, and a heartbreaking hour over in the storeroom trying to rearrange things so that there would be more space, Tim went out onto the square to get a little of the hot sun on his face, just for a minute, work his back muscles, and feel the hard exhaustion in his calves. There was the Queen of the Nile and her consort still. The kid had taken off his white shirt, tied it around his waist by the sleeves, and on his back someone had drawn a crude yin-yang circle in lipstick. The kid was swaying back and forth as the woman seemed to croon to him. Tim edged closer, trying not to look conspicuous, but he wanted to hear what the woman was singing, if she was singing. Again, she seemed to have a mysterious beauty denied by her features.

The song, when he got close enough to hear her thin piping voice, was not in any language Tim had ever heard, nor was the melody familiar. Tim edged away and then went back inside, grinning to himself. Valerie was getting a little competition in the lunatic sweepstakes.

Theo had forgotten all about Valerie. He did not remember who had drawn on his back in lipstick. He felt the heat of the new sunburn, but it did not bother him. His mind was filled by the beauty of the Queen. Nothing had seemed real for a long time, but now this woman was real, and he wanted to stay at her feet forever. And the King, her man, was encouraging. He told Theo that she was the reincarnated Hepshehut II, queen of Egypt, Pharoah actually, around three thousand B.C. But that she needed help, as we all need help.

"I think I have some money," Theo said.

"Oh, I don't use money," the Queen said, but the King said, "Give it to me. I take care of these things," and so Theo was un-burdened of his money, free at last.

"I feel better," he said, blinking into the sun.

"Yes," said the Queen.

"Yes," said the King.

A T first he had only wanted to get away from the others. They had frightened him, and although he was used to living with his fears, these awful men, these hoboes, inspired him with new levels of fear to overcome. He would get to the bus stop and hope nobody else was around. Then he would take the bus to the city and then catch another bus home. It was late. He hoped the "eight hits" he had taken by mistake would not screw him up too much. He had heard of people back in the sixties going crazy from the stuff. But you heard that about everything.

The street he was on did not lead to the square, but began to meander up into the hills. He did not remember climbing any hills before, but he kept going until he found a narrow street under big trees that seemed to head downhill. He felt all right now. The stars were clear in a warm sky, clear as a bell, clearer than a bell—he could almost hear the stars. The trees leapt up gigantic *plants*, he had not thought about it before, but redwoods were just plants after all, and he was tiny beneath them. He passed houses masked by fences, shrubs, dark mysterious growths, some of the houses with glowing yellow lights warmly flooding from windows or doorways, and once there was even a faint sound of music coming from nowhere, violins, a lot of them, rods of sound blueyellowgreenpinksound, oh, he had forgotten how painfully exquisite such sounds could be, and he had forgotten—

"I HAVE TO PISS!" he shouted. He giggled. No one cared. Why didn't he just piss and the hell with it? Take out his little old pecker and send a stream of piss arching into the electric blue . . . ha, here was the square, floating under its isolated lights, each lamp with its own blueyellow aura, each lamp singing a different tune, and he was in the middle of the square and it was deserted.

He stood with his hands raised in the air. He felt fine. He could piss later, his bladder the size of a football field, a stadium full of piss, slopping over in the earthquake. He laughed. There was no earthquake, or the bricks of the square would be popping up and flying around like mortar fragments.

"I'M PISSED, OFF!!" he yelled, but nobody answered. He was alone out there. Those fuckers stole his wallet and threw it, away, threw, it, away, over there, over that fence. He would have to find his wallet before the bus came down out of the sky, tiny bus to carry him away . . . the fence. The fence was easy. He hung on the fence smiling to himself. Then his anger returned and he vaulted over the fence and into a cushion of wonderful plants, soft like a bed of ferns, smelling like some kind of foreign candy. Then gravel. The gravel cut against the palms of his hands. He felt carefully for his wallet. It had to be around here somewhere.

Then he lost his temper, really lost it. He stood, flinging gravel, screaming words he did not even know. He ran for the fence but instead of vaulting it he slammed against it and fell back onto the gravel. He lay staring at the terrible stars, his tongue filling his mouth. He was gorged with hate, with rage. He wanted to explode into action, to rip, to kill. He got to his feet, both hands clutching gravel so hard it hurt. But he wanted pain.

One police car slid into the square swiftly, and the other one up to the bus stop. The two cops got out with their sticks and moved in on the corporation yard. These night police had plenty of experience and knew what they were doing. There was a howling drunk or something, spacecase, in the city yard, and they would get him and stick him in jail.

Theo was ready for them. He stood in the middle of the yard in starlight with his double fists of gravel. *"I'll kill you fuckers stole my wallet!*" he screamed. Then it became confusing. Somebody grabbed him around the waist from behind and he was in the bushes, the guy's breath hot on his ear, the guy's strong arms around him, pulling. Then they fell, and Theo landed hard in icy water—he could hear the gurgle of the stream—then the guy was pulling him wet splashing along into a dark terrifying place with loud gurgling echoes. Theo began to blubber, but the guy pinning him went "*Shh!*" and Theo kept quiet. They were down, down somewhere, water, a stream, light gone, darkness everywhere. Eventually as he sat wet, held from behind by the silent man whose beard he could feel and whose whiskey breath he could smell, he realized they were in some kind of tunnel under the street, a waterway, a creek, with an arch of concrete overhead. And he realized that the guy holding him had by some miracle gotten him away from the cops. The icy water had sobered him much, but still the LSD flooded his brain and he lay and let it happen.

After a while the other guy said, "It's okay, they must be gone. You make too goddamn much noise."

Theo recognized Nifty Nick as his benefactor.

"Nifty Nick," he said.

"You go get the hell out of here," Nifty Nick said. "Go that way."

Theo stumbled off down the creekbed under the arched concrete. He came out into starlight and then went under again, his feet icy went, the stones underfoot slippery. Eventually he found himself where he could pull himself up a rocky bank to ground level, and here he was in a lumberyard, stacks of lumber all over the place, and he got out of there and walked endlessly down an empty street, and then he was in the open, the sky above, rolling land under his feet. He kept walking because he did not know what else to do.

He woke up in the middle of a hot morning. He was under a bush, in the salt marsh, a couple of miles south of the town square. The acid still curled around the edges of his mind, but he knew where he was. He could see the mountain to the north and the long overarching highway bridge to the south, the bay, the hills.

But the thing was, he had no memory of who he was. Perhaps he did not care to remember.

Tɪᴍ was disturbed by what he saw as the corruption of the kid in the white shirt. The shirt was no longer white, of course, but stained and grimy. The kid never wore it except around his waist, and he was eighty-six from the depot by now, since he had no more money and he had tried to pull a fast one. Well, not such a fast one, but something they all tried from time to time. Small coffee was forty cents, and tradition (not management) had made a single refill free. You just came up and refilled your cup and nobody said anything.

Naturally, there were those who would rummage around in the trash bins and find a white plastic cup that hadn't been chewed on or ripped or otherwise made disgusting, and would come up to the counter and pour themselves free coffee all day long. The kid would not have been eightysixed for this common offence, but when caught by Dorothy, the whitehaired old woman, he bitched loudly, saying, "The coffee ought to be free!"

The old woman had no choice. "You better not come in here anymore," she said to him.

The kid looked around brighteyed, about to make some loud remark or other, but somehow the old woman had taken the steam out of him, and with an embarrassed nod and a mumbled, "I'm sorry," the kid left.

"I hated to do that," Dorothy said to Tim. "He's not a bad kid. Those crazy people messed him up."

They had indeed, and he was not the only one. Tim hated to see the young ones messed up, but he had no control over the square, and wanted none. But there was one kid out there, at the feet of the

Queen of the Nile, who really bothered Tim. Maybe it was a reflection on his own past—Tim had been plump as a boy, and had only gotten over it by, oddly, losing his faith in God and exercising furiously. This fat kid couldn't have been more than thirteen, probably less. He had shown up one day shirtless but wearing a loosely tied rep tie, and crude circles of rouge on his cheeks, as if to demonstrate that although he was not crazy yet, he had the spirit, and was willing to become crazy if anybody would show him how.

The shirtlessness was not exclusive among the followers of the Queen. Many on the square were stripping themselves in the increasing and highly unusual heat of the early summer. In desperate contrast were those who wore their wardrobes every day. One might see Milos in his rags, now wearing a dirty old red stocking cap, carrying his gnarled stick, his eyes hidden by a pair of garbage-can sunglasses, standing next to a man dressed only in cutoff jeans and bare feet. "Dressed in bare feet" was wrong, Tim knew, but that was how he thought of it: you put on your bare feet with your birthday suit.

Insanely, he wanted to say to Fahima, "Let's put on our birthday suits and run out into the square, ha ha!" But of course she would not get the joke. She was funny about the heat anyway, coming to work in a different cotton sweatshirt every day. "It makes me cool," she told him. He wondered how many of the expensive sweatshirts she had, pure cotton. Worker clothes were expensive these days.

Looking out through the window Tim could see the kid in the white shirt up dancing in front of the King and Queen, dancing crazy, while people watched and grinned or openly laughed. There were rumors that he was high on LSD all the time, that he was a rich kid from Los Angeles who had been brought here by a woman who had kidnapped him and then dumped him, but Tim did not believe that particular story. The LSD could be possible, the kid acted strangely enough. But they weren't all on LSD out there—there was something else in the air. Madness, as far as Tim was concerned.

Valerie was getting out of hand, too. Maybe he was jealous of the attention shifting over to the Queen of the Nile. Valerie had nothing but acid comments to make about the royal pair, if anybody asked him. But fewer and fewer people were paying attention to Valerie. He was becoming part of the landscape, there on his spot from dawn to dusk, working on his bed cover, throwing an occasional baleful glance toward the depot.

Then one afternoon when the heat was almost oppressive, somebody came along and parked in front of the depot, all the windows of his old Dodge open, his radio blaring rock music. The guy got out of his car dressed in a red bikini bathing suit, his sunburnt body covered with glistening red hairs, his head shaved, rills of sweat dripping off his body as he lazily ambled into the depot, leaving his radio running.

"That's awful," Valerie said to nobody. "He just leaves that loud radio on playing that disgusting music. Bothering people who don't want to be bothered." *Click click* went the needles.

When the man oozed redly out of the depot, clutching his bagel dog in one hand and his orange juice smoothie in the other, Valerie shouted over at him, "Turn down that stupid radio, please!"

The guy looked toward Valerie, obviously surprised. "Fuck you!" he shouted cheerfully, and took a bite of his bagel dog before shifting it to his other hand to open the door of his car.

Valerie threw down his work and got to his feet. "You turn DOWN that radio!" he shouted. Valerie went over to the guy, his eyes wild with anger. People were coming around and out of the depot to watch this wonderful diversion.

"You and who else, fuggin' faggot," the guy said, and put the bagel dog and smoothie down on his hood. His big meaty arms hung loosely, their big mauling fists half-clenched.

"Well, just *Piss* on *You!*" Valerie shouted and hit the guy right in the face. The guy went back but not down, surprise on his wide face. Then pleasure, as he grinned.

"Ah," he said. "Ah, ah, ah." He moved toward Valerie, bringing up his fists in the boxer's stance, but before he could actually start boxing, Valerie hit him again, on the nose, and bright blood spurted out and down the man's hairy front. The man looked at his own gushing blood, amazed, and then his face went white and he fell to the ground in a dead faint. Valerie reached into his car and turned off the radio.

"People should have a little consideration," he said with great dignity, and went back to his work. There was a small burst of applause from the onlookers. The cops came and got Valerie about ten minutes after the man had picked himself up (no one came forward to help him), gotten into his car, and driven off. The cops were not easy on Valerie. They spread-eagled him across the hood, cuffed his hands in back, rammed him into the backseat of the copcar, and rode off, their faces daring anybody to make any kind of protest.

Nobody did.

Tᴵᴹ should have gone home at five but it was almost six and he was still at the depot, his own sweatsmell beginning to nauseate him, unable to leave because Alfreda, one of his employees, had complained of faintness and left early. So here he was in the slot, handing out soft drinks and coffee, *lattes* and espressos, and collecting money that was warm and greasy to the touch, cursing Alfreda's insouciance (or whatever it was—she had called in sick or left early so many times on so many excuses) and wishing it wasn't so damned hot.

As if by magic the heat broke that afternoon. A customer came in wearing a satin jacket, and Tim kidded with him until the guy said, "It's cold as hell in the city," and Tim looked up at the serried tops of the redwoods to the west and saw the white fog blowing in. At last! And just then the kid Tim had called in to replace Alfreda showed up, little Terry. Tim grinned and took off his red apron. Outside on the square he could see that all the seminude people were gone. Also gone were the King and Queen and their admirers, or observers, or whatever they were. In fact, the only person out there was Milos, the new wind ruffling him as he stood silently in the very center of the square, not moving.

In a few minutes, the time it took Tim to go back into the tiny employees' room and get his attaché case, the temperature outside dropped twenty degrees, and all the people in the depot were jabbering happily. Tim said goody-bye and walked out onto the square, feeling the sharp chill wind gratefully as he walked over to his car, parked next to the fence to the old city yard, its nose in some Scotch broom. Tim found a pink ticket flapping under his windshield wip-

er. He should have parked further down, where there were no meters, or at least kept coming out to plug the meter. He got two or
three tickets a month, and they added up. Lazy.

Tim opened the door and felt the heat billow out past him. He
waited for the inside to cool, his hand on the top of the car's open
door, thinking absolutely nothing at all, when Fahima appeared on
the other side of the hood, smiling at him expectantly. She was
wearing a turquoise cotton sweatshirt, and so, he thought inanely,
she was probably warm enough. He was so surprised to see her that
he stood and stared until she laughed at him.

"Did I frighten you?" she asked.

"I just thought you were long gone," he said. "Home with Hassie." Her dark hair, usually tied back while she worked, was now
loose and luxuriant, ruffling across her face, making her more beautiful than ever.

She had been shopping across the square and had seen Tim. "I
just wanted to say hello," she said. "Oh, you look so tired!"

"I *am* tired," Tim admitted, and then smiled to show that it didn't
matter. Now would be a perfect time to ask her to have a drink. They
could go across to the local tavern and have a drink, talk, and then
go home, him to his wife, she to her husband. Tim reddened, just
thinking about it, and she was quick to notice.

"Are you all right?"

"Yes, I'm fine. Are you in a hurry?"

"I have to go to market, and then home to fix supper," she said.
"The freeway this time of night." She and Hassan lived a couple of
miles up the freeway. So did Tim, but in another town.

"I hate the thought of getting out there, even with this fine summer fog cooling things off," he said. What a ridiculous figure of a
man he was! He couldn't even ask this nice friend for a drink. Some
guy! One hell of a civilized gent.

They stood on opposite sides of Tim's old car, smiling at each other, neither speaking, neither moving. Then it was overcast and really cold, after the eighty-degree temperature of that afternoon. Tim shivered and said, "Well, I guess the car's cooled off."

"I see you in morning," she said. "I just wanted to say hello." Tim watched her walking away. Why hadn't he offered to walk her to her car? Why hadn't he asked her to sleep with him? Why hadn't he enlisted in the Marines twenty years ago? Fah.

He was disgusted with himself. But he did not know if his disgust came from the fact that he had not had the guts to ask her to have a drink with him (etcetera), or from the fact that he was an old married man acting just exactly like an old married man.

Milos yelled something at Fahima as she walked, shaking his stick and stamping on the bricks, but she ignored him. She could take care of herself, Tim thought. She doesn't need me.

What a strange thought. Tim got in his car and shut the door too hard. He started the engine, and letting it warm, fooled with the radio, turning up the volume. Jazz, no, rock'n'roll, no, country, no, ah, early music, Vivaldi, sing, you fucking violins, sing! For I am in a piss-cutter of a mood!

The fog rolled over the hills, thick and white among the dark redwoods, making everything look like a Japanese print. Tim drove off into the fog, broken-down samurai with a stirring spoon. Home to the hearth, home to his honey, home to the emptiness that just hadn't been there before.

THE white shirt had been enough to take the chill off when the nights had been warm and clear. Now with the fog Theo could not get comfortable. He had meant to ask somebody if there was a place he could stay, but when the fog came everybody he knew to speak to drifted off and he was left alone again. He was not hungry anymore. The hunger seemed to pass, and of course there was plenty of water. This was how things should be. People did not need all the things they thought they needed. And people did not need drugs. He had not taken any drugs lately, yet everything seemed edged with flame, expectancy. He wandered around, holding himself as he shivered. He knew he could always go to the police, but he did not want to do that. They would put him in jail at least for the night, but they could not take him home because he did not know where home was. He had no home. He had no memories of anything like a home. He did not even know his own name. Lately people had been calling him Oscar. That was fine. He would use that name until he found another.

For Oscar, then, the night seemed endless. He went to the park but it was ominous and cold, and he left shivering, almost running back to the town square. The lights were on in the depot, promising warmth, but he had been kicked out of there. Music poured from the lit cocktail bar across the street, but he did not want to go in there and be thrown out. He was not old enough, he knew, although he did not know his age, exactly.

Walking south down the tree-lined street he looked for a car he could get into and curl up. He tried a lot of doors before he found one that would open. He got into the old car, smelling the upholstery and stale tobacco. He curled up on the backseat and waited for the shivering to stop, but it didn't. He clutched his knees to his chest and felt his whole body tremble. It was all right. Pretty soon he would be asleep.

But that did not happen. After a while he could not stand it, and so he got out of the car and started down the long street again. Walking fast made him slowly warm up. In a few blocks he was swinging right along, his body sweetly warm, his mind misty, the cold wind cutting against his cheek. As he moved gradually out into the open the wind got worse and the fog blew around him in a thick solid mass like smoke. He was walking down the bike path now, the highway running along the edge of the salt marsh. He remembered that place. He had slept there, only it had been a warm night. He followed a little path down into the marsh and the other bike path along the old railroad right-of-way. But the wind here was really fierce, and he realized he would have to turn around and go back, where the redwoods partially shielded him from the wind. His legs hurt, his feet were sore, his stomach muscles painfully tight.

But this was freedom, was it not? Well, he did not want to think about that. He did not want to think at all, and it was easy not to think, now that he knew what he was. An insect. Nothing more. Just an insect.

But he had to admit it was no fun being an insect. Crawling along, brokenbug, waiting for the final footstep that crushes him into the sidewalk. Maybe he could find Nifty Nick. Maybe Nick had some place down there by the creek that he could share. Nick would share with him. Nick was a great guy, no matter what he looked like in the daylight.

He walked and walked until he was dizzy with exhaustion, but he could not stop because if he stopped the cold would get him. And so at last he came up to the lumberyard. There was the cyclone fence to climb, only about six feet high. Right here next to the gate the fence was all tangled with a rosebush growing all over it, he could smell the roses in the dark. Over the gate itself they had some barbed wire strung, so he went down a ways to where some lumber was stacked inside the fence and made it easy for him to get over. Inside, the gravel underfoot made loud noise as he walked toward the bank of the creek. Crackle, crackle. Nick should be able to hear that, he thought, and scraped his feet deliberately.

"Nick?" he asked of the night.

No answer. It was about six feet down to the stream. The wall was just rocks, easy to climb down. But he fell anyway, luckily landing on a sandbank next to the water. He did not want to get wet, it would be too cold, too cold. . . He had knocked the air out of himself, so he lay on his side breathing, waiting for Nick to miraculously appear and take him into the warmth. "Nick?" he asked, rasping. "Nick, *help*. . ."

No Nick. He was getting cold again, freezing cold, and he thought about the day bringing its heat, how he would lie in the heat sucking it into his body, and hot hot sun sending burning rays into his skin. Ah, but not yet. Now it was just too cold to lie there thinking. He painfully got to his feet and walked on the soft sand upstream to where the tunnel under the street was, that would lead from the lumberyard to the other place, where Nick must be.

In the dark of the tunnel he got his feet wet. It was like ice, he thought. Got to get these shoes and socks off and dry. Or what? Or what? He tried to remember. Something bad happened to your feet in the snow. Gang Green.

"Nick? Nick?"

No Nick.

He began to cry. The tears were hot then cold against his face. As he cried, he remembered who he was. He had never really forgotten. He was not Oscar the fool, Oscar the idiot with lipstick all over his body, Oscar the plaything of the King. The King didn't even talk to him anymore, and got a disgusted put-upon look on his face when Oscar came toward him anymore, no, not Oscar. Theo. Theodore. No, they won't call you Teddy because you are not a teddy bear. No, the name is Theo. He remembered now that he hated his parents and they didn't like him much either. He would have to go home to them, but maybe only to kill them. Even as he cried, he laughed. He could not kill his parents. They might kill him, but he would not kill them.

"Nick?" No Nick.

There was nothing else for him to do. He sat with his back against the concrete retaining wall, the stream gurgling at his feet. He had violent episodes of shivering, and he held himself so hard his fingernails cut into his arms. He felt his feet go numb, but there was nothing he could do about it. Pinned down by enemy fire. He would have to stay there. Eventually he forgot all he had remembered. It was easier to let the numbness take control of him. The numbness would protect him, even make him a little warm.

But it did not, and the night passed terribly. By grey light he had to make a tremendous effort just to get to his feet. Everything was icy stiff and painful. Twice he fell back trying to climb up out of the waterway, and hurt himself both times. But at last he was out of the yard and staggering across the square. The garbage cans, he thought. But as he got near them a little man dressed in rags and carrying a stick started shouting at him. He had seen this man before but now he was frightened by him. He started to go back, his heart cold, when the old woman opened the back door to the depot and motioned to him. After he got inside, feeling the delicious warmth, she said, "You look like you could use a cuppa coffee, siddown." He sat, trying to say that he did not have any money, but no words would come out of his mouth. She set the hot coffee in front of him, and then a paper plate with a fresh hot croissant on it, butter melting over the top of it. Suddenly the smell of it made him dizzy with hunger.

"Here's three bucks," the old woman said. "You get on that bus and get the hell out of here. I see you again, I'll rap you on the head."

She watched him cross the square to the bus stop and next time she looked he was gone. Nobody ever saw him around there again.

For days a deep, seemingly endless sea of fog hung over the ocean and the hills west of town, leaving the mountain invisible and the redwoods black and wet with mist. Everything was cold. Dorothy, the old woman, hated getting out so early each morning, but it was better than her days off, when she might just lie in bed awake from 4:00 A.M., just lie there until her butt ached so much she had to get up and make coffee for herself. Much better to just haul up out of bed, dress in the blind, stumble down the hundred steps and go to work before she was even awake yet. The problem in the heavy summer fog was that the steps and the railing got wet and very slippery. This is how the old woman had hurt her tailbone, bump bump bump down the wet dark steps like some comedy routine, her yellin' her head off. . . So now she was pretty careful.

When it was cold like this there wasn't much early business, and so she could relax, gettin' everything in order, money out of the safe and counted into the register, water heating in the espresso machine and the coffee makers, soup heatin' up in the big kettles, tomatoes sliced and wedged, lettuce fresh and ready, fruits cut up for the salads, the place gradually gettin' warm, good jazz music on the radio. The old woman liked her jazz music, but she liked rock'n'roll, too. She liked it all, when it came to music.

Best of all she liked Fahima. She had never met anybody she liked so much, and between the two women for the last months a strong indivisible friendship had built up, to where Dorothy loved Fahima as much or more than she loved her own children and grandchildren, scattered all over the East and visited but seldom. Dorothy was a long-ago runaway from the domestic life. A real old dropout, she liked to say. Marijuana madness had set her free of a stultifying life as a businessman's wife, and she left him with a stack of stocks and bonds this thick, and the hell with him. She wanted nothing. She could make her own way, and she did.

At first when she heard the new girl was Iranian she thought, Oh, shit, another one a those, but Fahima on her first day at work won Dorothy over. She did it by bein' modest, soft-spoken, and a very hard worker, always doin' somethin', never quite idle, polite to everybody, big and strong, beautiful as a big cat, always willin' to see the humor in a fucked-up situation, and sayin' things like, "Oh, Dorothy, you must help me to learn!" Ah, what a girl!

And her and Tim, God. Dorothy had never seen such an obvious case of made-for-each-other, which is the only way she could put it because she didn't think they were really in love, just threatenin'. Because they were both good people, and in Dorothy's mind, good people did not betray their husbands and wives. In a way it was kind of sad, because in the old woman's mind, Tim and Fahima deserved each other.

Dorothy had never worked for a boss like Tim. She had been suspicious at first (as she was with nearly everybody) and grouched around, her lower lip out, her shoulders stooped, lettin' him take over if that's what he wanted. She figured that maybe because he'd owned his own place and lost it he was maybe too good for this shitty job and would be a prick to work for. But Tim had been so quiet and willin' to learn, and was so good about doin' shit jobs instead a takin' somebody off somethin' else, he was so honest, so good-humored, pretty soon he had everybody, even Dorothy, workin' twice as hard, humpin' right along, just for him.

She went to the back door and looked out at the windswept

square. Nobody out there this cold morning. There was time, so she took a half-smoked joint out of her apron pocket and lit it with her Bic lighter, stepping outside to puff and rest a moment.

"Drugs! You are taking drugs!" Milos shouted at her, spit flyin' everywhere.

"Aw, fuck you," she said, and went back inside. Imagine a bum like that talkin' to her like that!

Tim was so funny, really, about women. It was one of the reasons she liked him so much. He was punctilious. Absolutely. He would not lay a finger on one of his employees, not just because he was a married man, but because it was wrong, immoral, to take advantage of girls when their money was at stake. Pull that shit and God would come down and strike you dead. Oh, he didn't believe in God, so somethin' worse, some kinda swarm a demons or somethin'. Anyway, no matter whether the girls came on to him or not he would leave them strictly alone, none of that heavy-handed kiddin' everybody hated, and no fatherly horseshit.

So Fahima, due any minute now, would wait for Tim, not standin' around waitin' but Dorothy knew. She was *waitin'* for him, cause when he got there around seven-thirty Fahima would just brighten up, that was the only word for it, brighten up. They were both tall and Dorothy short, so it was quite a comedy if all three of them crowded into the little kitchen together, Dorothy duckin' around, Tim and Fahima tryin' to keep their hands off each other even though the very sparrows outside the window knew they wanted each other so bad they could taste it.

Ah, what a shame about Fahima's husband, Hassie the Handsome. And he was handsome, too, just like Errol Flynn standin' in a posthole. Growin' a belly, losin' some hair, you could see what he'd look like later, great guy, so in love with his wife, Dorothy speculated, that he'd go back to that fuckin' Iran and get his ass shot off, just for her. He came on like a dedicated revolutionary, but Dorothy thought, yeah, but would he be so dedicated without Fahima to inspire him? You could tell the way he looked at her that even after five years of marriage he still loved her desperately. Desperately but hopelessly, she thought, because Fahima did not love him back. She was fond of him, very fond, but that was not the same, now, was it? Not anything like the same.

She didn't treat him bad or say bad things about him, she just didn't love him. Poor Hassie. What must it be like to be married to such a woman, such an incredible woman, and know in your heart that she does not love you? Dorothy's sympathy went out to Hassan. But Fahima she loved.

Tim and his wife were a whole other kettle of fish. Dorothy did not know Tim's wife very well. She had come in for lunch a couple of times and been introduced, and damn her soul but what Dorothy saw was an older version of Fahima, tall, darkly beautiful, wonderful humor about the mouth and eyes. But. Older, a dozen years older. And bulging a little under her clothes. And there was something in her eyes, too, something Dorothy would not put a word to, and though Dorothy knew nothing of Tim and Claire's courtship, she could see one of those deals where the woman just sort of moves into the man's life inertly and lets him carry the ball. "I love you, I'm helpless, do what you please." Uh huh. But Dorothy liked her, and it was too bad.

There was a rapping at the front door. *Rap rap rap!* Like the emperor or somethin' was out there. "We're still closed," she said. She looked out through the glass. There stood a young man, his head cocked, thick dirty glasses, Hawaiian shirt, little crooked smile as he pointed his finger at the clock inside, indicating that it was actually one minute after seven, and Dorothy was late in opening.

Another nut, she thought, and opened the door. "Aren't you cold?" she asked him as he stood at the narrow counter and waited for her to pour his coffee.

"Ah, cold," he said. "But now I'm in here, so it's all right. Are *you* cold?" he asked anxiously, as if he knew her.

"Not no more," she said, and went into the kitchen to get away from him.

Piper, Zeno, and Victor were properly amused by the new nut, although all three admitted that he lacked the color or style of Valerie or the Queen of the Nile. On this particular morning the fog was low to the ground and hung white in the trees as if stuck there. Piper had on a hooded grey sweatshirt, hood tight around his head, cigarette in his mouth, giving him the appearance of an explorer. He kept his hands in the front warmer of the sweatshirt, his white plastic cup of coffee steaming on the fender of Zeno's Mercedes.

In the very next car sat the King and the Queen, having their morning coffee from one big cup shared between them. Strange things hung from the rearview mirror, and the car was filled with blankets, clothing, and utensils, a living junkpile. Piper kept his back to them as he spoke through slitted lips:

"What I want to know is, why doesn't she make the fog go away? Huh? What about her magical powers, huh? I ask you."

Victor said, "She got rid of Valerie, didn't she? You ask too much. Be content with small favors."

Zeno was amused. "I hate to think of poor Valerie up there in county jail."

"Yeah, makin' money hand over fist," said Piper.

"So to speak," said Victor.

They were not sure Valerie was in the county jail. Nobody really knew what had happened to him. But it was a valid assumption, as Zeno remarked.

Right now Zeno himself was deep in a personal debate, an age-old debate, but one very close to his heart. Zeno was thinking of becom-

ing an artist. He was not sure what medium he would employ, but
the writing medium seemed most attractive, because Zeno already
knew how to write, and would only have to apply himself to the subject matter he chose to write about. No music lessons or painting in-
structions to endure before he got down to the nitty-gritty.

But the trick was to create your art and make good money at the
same time. Zeno did not see why it could not be that way, if you
planned carefully. The thing was to make great art that would also
make good money. That was the trick.

"Sounds good to me," Victor said.

"I mean, it seems absolutely crazy to me to sit in some attic somewhere and write your ass off about something people don't want to
read about. If you're going to bust your hump you should at least get
paid for it," Zeno reasoned.

"Perfectly reasonable," Victor said.

"What's the Nobel Prize worth?" Piper asked humorously.

"Almost two hundred grand," Zeno said.

"Worth shooting for," Victor said.

"Go ahead, make fun of me," Zeno said with a nice smile. "You'll
laugh when I get rich."

A voice spoke up behind them, surprising all three:

"It would be nice to be rich, but it really isn't important, is it?"

They turned to see that the new nut, the guy from inside with the
thick glasses and the yellow and green Hawaiian shirt, had joined
them without asking permission. Guy about thirty, thirty-five,
cocked his head to one side like a bird listening for worms.

The three stared at this uninvited intrusion, but the guy didn't
seem to get the message.

"I couldn't help overhearing part of your conversation," he said.
"I think it's important to write about things, but what we really need
is more positive action, don't you think?" His hands were jammed
down into his pants pockets.

"Are you cold? Why don't you go back inside?" Victor asked rudely. The man grinned at him, head cocked again, and said nothing. The three turned so that he would be outside their circle, but he moved, too, and included himself in.

"I think we have to work on this business of no more wars," he said. "I think really everything else has to wait, don't you think? I mean the urgency is clear, isn't it? Don't you agree?"

After looking at each other with raised eyebrows at this breach of manners, Victor said coldly, "Of course. Thank you for informing us."

"Oh, you're very welcome. I have a plan, of course. I wouldn't just talk about doing something without having something of my own to do."

"Perfect sense," said Zeno, draining his *latte*. "I got to go," he said to the others.

"No, wait," said Victor. "This could be important." Victor was known for his vicious sense of humor, so Zeno paused, expectant, his hand on the door of his car.

"What's your plan?" Victor asked the guy seriously. The guy grinned and said, "Oh, I have it all drawn up, you would have to see my plans, but in general the idea is to ship all weapons, especially atomic weapons, to some other planet. I think Venus would be the best, because it's so hot there nobody could go down and get the stuff back."

"I'd love to see those plans," Victor said.

"I thought you were going to say something funny," Zeno said, opening his car door in disappointment. Next thing, Piper and the new guy were standing there together, just the two of them, the King and the Queen watching them from behind their dirty windshield. This inspired Piper. That woman made him nervous anyway.

"What's your name?" he asked the grinning stranger.

"Oh, I don't have a name," he said. "I gave up my name a long time ago. It wasn't me, anyway. But I have a nickname people call me if they want to. It's not much of a nickname, it's supposed to be an insult, but you know me, I don't much take offense. People call me Four Eyes. The glasses, you know. Lots of people wear glasses, but I guess mine are pretty thick, make my eyes look pretty big, so people call me Four Eyes."

"Okay, Four Eyes," Piper said, making a gesture toward the King and the Queen, "I'd like to introduce you to the Queen of the Nile and her consort, known as the King. You guys ought to have a lot in common." With this Piper whirled and moved off toward the depot, bowing to an imaginary audience, hearing ghost applause.

"Hello, Your Majesty," said Four Eyes to the dirty windshield. "Should I call you that? Is that all right?"

I N the night the fog blew away and the moon could be seen rising full. The breeze lessened and the air warmed, stars made themselves known, and Orion the great giant marched across the sky. Four Eyes smiled and put his hands behind his head, looking up at the sky with great contentment. He had set up camp in the salt marsh, right out in the middle, in a copse of small trees near a trail that lead into the heart of the marsh. South he could see the overarching highway bridge with its constant stream of moving lights, testimony to the endless pulse of American humanity; the small bay lay flat waiting for the streak of moonshine that was to come, and Four Eyes waited, too, patiently; perhaps not as patiently as the bay, but calm and easy enough. He smiled to himself again. This was a nice camp. There was the mountain now, a darkness against the stars. A nice camp.

He had come into town through the salt marsh, walking up the bike path that had been laid over the old railroad tracks, his pack light on his back, his staff in hand. The staff he had found near an old hobo camp well south of here, a long stick a little less than two inches thick and just over five feet long, bark long ago peeled off and the wood polished down and begrimed by horny unknown hands. It felt good in Four Eyes' hand as he walked. He had walked thus into town and past, up a fire trail onto the mountain, and then, remembering the marsh, went back down and found the little copse of trees, bay or laurel or something, with no recent human footprints in the sandy soil. He found a good place to conceal his bedroll and pack under a shrub that was tight to the ground. The only drawback had been the fog and wind, and now they had gone.

Soon he fell into a contented sleep.

The next morning Four Eyes awakened in time to lazily watch the sky turn from lead grey to blue as the sun rose clear where the moon had risen the night before; the moon now pale and low over the mountain. It was going to be a nice warm day. He got up, rolled up his bedroll, tucked his things away, and walked the two miles to the depot for his morning coffee.

After coffee and some interesting conversations with various people, he left the depot, got his stick from where he had hidden it outside, and walked again up a fire trail onto the mountain. For the first uphill twenty minutes or so he was in chill shade, but then he broke out into the open and it was warm, the day beginning to get hot. He did not particularly mind either hot or cold weather. There were people running up and down the mountain, huff huff huff they would go past him, never meeting his eye, never speaking, even if he said, "Good morning!" or, "Nice day!" He was used to that— joggers seemed to concentrate inward while they were running. But once a man with a dark mustache and a heavy-looking yellow sweat suit stopped and glared at him, the sweat running in rivers from his hair down his face. His eyes were forbidding. Four Eyes stopped, too, and smiled at the man.

"Good morning!" said Four Eyes.

"You shouldn't carry that weapon on these trails," the jogger said.

"What weapon?"

"That big stick. We've had trouble up here with people accosting women in the trail."

"This stick?" Four Eyes asked.

"It's a weapon," the man said forbiddingly, and ran off down the trail.

"Oh well," said Four Eyes. He threw his staff into the manzanita beside the trail and went on without it. He did not want to seem to be carrying a weapon, what with his attitude toward weapons. Before they turned the earth into a tiny sun. He hiked on, light sweat cooling his body. Here were two girls on a rock, resting. He smiled and said hello and went over to them, but they got up and ran down the trail without meeting his eyes. Oh, he was used to that.

Later he went off the trail down through some pine trees and found a little pond, too shallow to bathe in, but there were late spring pollywogs and some tiny green frogs around the edges, the little frogs swimming kickstroke. There were even some of the frogs in the grass beside the water, among swarms of gnats. Breakfast time, he thought with amusement at the tiny emerald things. It was a nice pond. But they would blow it out of existence if they could. And only Four Eyes seemed to have a plan to stop them. He saw raccoon prints in the mud and thought that the frogs and pollywogs must make an easy breakfast for the animals. He had eaten pollywogs himself, more than once. The trick was to swallow them whole.

"Good-bye," he said to everything, knowing contentedly that nothing understood him, and went back up to the trail. After a few hundred yards uphill the trail took a curve and suddenly he could see for miles. The mountain fell away sharply, and the town sat below under its own faint blue haze; beyond it the marsh, the bay, the freeway, everything. He sat on a rock and looked at the view for a long time. This might be my place, he thought.

In an hour he was back in the depot, drinking coffee and munching on a sweet roll. There were conversations all around him, and he openly listened, smiling whenever he caught anyone's eye. He was always looking for people to talk to about his plan to get rid of the weapons.

From eavesdropping he learned that the man outside sitting on the curb across the street had just reappeared, having been gone for several days. Four Eyes was curious: Who was this person, and why sit on the curb?

BACK outside Four Eyes could feel the heat rising. Even after the fog, it was going to be a very hot day. As he approached Valerie he could see sweat on the seated man's nearly shaven head, big drops in some places, rills of shining moisture running down and under his collar. Valerie was frowning at his work, and did not look up when Four Eyes hunkered down beside him.

"May I ask you a question?" Four Eyes said.

"Well, I suppose you're going to ask it anyway," Valerie said without looking at Four Eyes.

"I was just wondering why you sat on the curb."

Valerie looked now, with his eyebrows raised, ready to tell the man to go away. The Hawaiian shirt, which he had seen coming, was really ugly and, now he saw, dirty, too. The man's big round glasses were dirty, and so were his feet in his old sandals. But for some reason Valerie found himself answering:

"You know, while I was gone the gardener planted a lot of flowers here in my place. I think he wants to get rid of me. First they were primroses, but now pansies. Look."

Four Eyes looked. There were several nice-looking bunches of yellow and purple pansies behind Valerie, in fresh dirt.

"I had to spend time moving them," Valerie explained.

"I have plans for getting rid of all weapons," Four Eyes said. "I don't have the plans with me, but it's really pretty simple." He explained about sending all weapons, starting with the atomic ones, to Venus by rocket ship.

"That would be a good idea," Valerie said without any apparent interest. Four Eyes stayed squatted down smiling at Valerie for a few minutes, but there was no more conversation. The heat was getting intense, although nothing like the terrible heat of other parts of the country.

Finally, Four Eyes got to his feet and went back over to the depot. In the bottom of the busing cart they kept the newspapers that people bought, read, and left behind. After he got another cup of coffee he squatted in front of the busing cart and assembled a newspaper for himself. As he stood again he was bumped sharply by somebody coming in the back door.

"Excuse me," he said, and turned to see a small young woman whose eyes did not see him as she brushed past. There was something about her that interested him, and as he sat at his little table by the back door he watched her. She got a cup of coffee and went to a table and sat looking at nothing. She was pretty, with light brown hair, a pale yellow tee shirt and jeans rolled up almost to the knees, small bare feet, toenails that had been painted crimson and then chipped and gotten dirty. She was pretty, yes, but without expression. His heart went out to her immediately. He could see that she was a lost soul. But he had never had any luck talking to young women. Take the ones on the rock up on the mountain, a perfect example.

He looked at her for a long time, hoping to catch her eye so that he could smile at her with reassurance, but it never happened, and after a while she got up, walked past him, put her empty cup in the busing tray with the others, and went out the back door, all without meeting his eye.

Four Eyes read his paper. It was filled with confirmation. Things may not have been getting worse, but they were certainly not getting any better. He tried talking to a few people about what was in the newpaper, but no one seemed interested. Some got irritated when he broke into their conversations or their own quiet reading of the paper, others seemed to think he was funny. Yet he still felt that this might be a good place for him to settle for a while. It was not entirely negative; the woman behind the counter, a tall, very beautiful dark-skinned woman, had smiled at him when she refilled his coffee cup. And the people coming and going seemed a mix of all types of humanity.

After a few days he had more or less established his beachhead. The little table by the back door was almost always open for him, since most people did not like being brushed by those coming or going. The employees were nice to him, some of the customers had begun to nod or say hello. He was fast becoming a regular, and he liked the feeling.

When he was not sitting in the depot or out back on the square, he walked. He walked all through the salt marsh on both sides of the small bay, at high tide and low, seeing the dozen or so white egrets all standing in a clump waiting for the tide with its influx of tiny fish; seeing the great blue heron, over three feet tall, standing imperiously nearby, refusing to join the egrets but waiting for his breakfast all the same, long stabber of a beak, yellow glaring eye; seeing the terns squealing and wheeling high in the air above the little bay, then to drop like mad things into the water; seeing more every time he looked, slowly, gradually accustoming himself to his new temporary home. He walked on the mountain, beginning to learn its own varieties, its own birds and animals, rocks and flowers. Much of the time he was alone, as if he owned the earth. But sometimes there would be the bicyclers, the joggers, and the other walkers.

He saw the girl often at the depot now. Her name was Patty, and she had come to town right about the same time as Four Eyes. With the return of the heat wave the square was covered with people, either sunning themselves or jealously guarding their shady spots. She was one of the ones who liked the shade, and was often sitting on one of the wooden chairs under the arches outside the depot back door. He did not know why she interested him. He liked to talk to young women, perhaps that was it.

And the depot was still good for some depot things, even though the trains didn't run anymore and the buses stopped a block away. Four Eyes used the big sink in the restroom to shave with his straight razor, and sometimes if he got there early enough to have the restroom to himself he would take a sponge bath, using depot soap and depot paper towels. He would come out with his face freshly shaved and washed, his longish hair combed and wet, even his glasses might be freshly clean. But as he sat drinking coffee and reading his morning's newspaper he would finger his glasses until they were smeared and dirty again.

Sometimes he would bring his roll of papers, his plan, and work on it sitting at his little table, making remarks, drawings, and doodles with an old ballpoint pen. If he showed his plans to anybody the comment would often be that his handwriting was impossible to read, and that his drawings, usually of rocket ships, were old-fashioned and silly.

"Oh," he might say, "I'm no writer or artist. The idea's the thing."

He wanted to show Patty his plans, but was shy about it. She seemed to make herself at home around the depot, and was there sometimes all through the day and into the evening. He wondered how she lived, where she slept. Many of the people around here didn't have any real homes; some slept in cars or in the woods or had little special places on other people's property that they were allowed to use. There weren't nearly as many women hanging around as men, and she was the only young and pretty one aside from the high school girls who came around in the afternoons and evenings to be with the boys who used the square as their meeting place. He had seen her smile now and then, even laugh, but once when she was laughing at something somebody had said Four Eyes tried to catch her eyes and share the laugh, but she would not lock eyes with him. It was too bad.

But there were lots of other things happening all around him, and he took an interest in much of it. For example, the Queen of the Nile.

One morning for some reason there were a lot of people out in front of the depot, standing around or leaning on parked cars. Valerie was across the street hard at work, Victor, Zeno, and Piper were enjoying their morning before the heat drove them their separate ways, the King and the Queen were leaning on their own car, the King talking quietly to Patty, who seemed very interested in what he was saying. Four Eyes leaned on the drinking fountain in the shade of the tree outside the kitchen window, sipping cool water from an old plastic cup. The King's wolfish face worried him. The man looked hard and cold. He wondered what they were talking about, when suddenly Piper began talking loudly and gesturing, as if to an audience somewhere in the middle of the street.

Maybe it was the girl Patty who inspired Piper. Or the heat was bothering him. Nobody ever found out. Piper seemed excited and nervous as he made what he thought was a string of brilliant jokes, all at the expense of the King and especially the Queen.

"I don't get it," Piper said, working his mouth in quick smile moves and pacing up and down in front of his friends. "Here I made plans for a trip to ancient Egypt, based on this woman's representations, and what happens? Nothing. Now listen to them. The young lady is being asked to travel along, I don't know, will it be a big bus, and pull up to the square and everybody who's signed her pictures climbs aboard and the fuckin' bus just takes off into the sky? I don't get it?"

"Bend over, you will," Zeno said with an amused wink at Victor.

Piper ingored Zeno. He moved close to the Queen. "Ma'am, I'm sorry to intrude, but do you remember talking to me about going on your special tour? Things are getting pretty boring around here, I was wondering when the trip was scheduled. I have to make plans, you know. I can't just pick up and leave. I have obligations, people who have to be told where I'm gonna be."

"You could leave town at the drop of a hat," Victor said.

"I ask you, ladies and gentlemen of the audio radience, what am I to make of this? Am I being led on? Is there to be no trip?"

"If she said you'll go, you'll go," the King said in his gravelly voice. He obviously did not like what Piper was doing. But so what? The Queen merely leaned against her fender and toyed with her long, dirty, picture-laden skirt, her eyes downcast, a little smile on her mouth. How could she dress so heavily in such weather? She was not only wearing the long dress, but there were long petticoats under it, and she had on this little short black velvet-looking jacket, dusty-looking, a couple of magazine pictures of scenes of ancient Egypt pinned to it, scribbled all over, the woman was clearly nuts.

Piper spoke to her directly. "Ma'am, Madam Queen? Hello? I know you're out there, I can hear you breathing."

"Piper," Victor said with a tone of restraint in his voice.

"Just a minute, just a minute," Piper said. He seemed even more agitated than before. Patty watched him flatly, her eyes showing nothing. If Piper was trying to impress her, he did not seem to be succeeding.

"Look, lady, what I want to know is, do I have a reservation for the trip, or not? And if so, when do we go? Is there an orchestra aboard? Will there be dancing? Good food? Do we have to dress for dinner?"

The Queen finally looked up at Piper, her shy quiet face untouched by the heat. "Would you like to go?" she asked quietly.

"Would I like to go? I ask you," he said to his imaginary audience. "What have I been talking about all morning? Of course I'd like to go. I'd like to go right away. This place is getting too crowded. Too many characters around. And it's getting too hot, not that it won't be hot in old Egypt, but there's the river to cool off in, no? Yes?"

"When would you like to go?" the Queen asked in her mild voice.

"When? Why, right away! Oh, don't just send me off right this instant, I have to go home and pack, make arrangements for my dog, sublet the apartment, you know, all the little petty details of travel. And travelers' checks, I would need to get some of those. So I would need at least, let's see, oh, a couple of hours before departure. Can you arrange that?"

This time the King spoke, with irritation, almost anger. "You'll go," he said.

"Well, gosh, I better get home and pack, then, huh?" He looked at his friends for approval, sweat shining on his high forehead. It all broke up then, Zeno getting into his car and driving off, Victor drifting away, Piper heading up to his apartment.

The next morning, when Piper didn't show up, Victor said, "I hope he's enjoying the place."

"What place?" asked Zeno.

"Ancient Egypt," Victor said with a straight face. Zeno laughed, but nobody around there ever saw Piper again.

Tim told himself many times that he couldn't be bothered with what happened to the people who came and went; they were not his concern. You just couldn't let them get to you. You had to harden yourself, like a doctor has to harden himself to terrible things. But still, the young woman called Patty was a special case. Oh, he knew. He did not delude himself. If she had been a young man he wouldn't have paid her any special attention, and had she been older or less pretty, he might not have cared. But none of that mattered, because he *did* care, and that was that.

It was pretty obvious to Tim that she got her money, at least part of it, from men. She wasn't a hooker—at least he hoped she wasn't a hooker—but she seemed to have a way of pairing up with the most obviously lonely men who hung around downtown. Let one stand for them all, a tall thin red-cheeked man with large flapping ears and a beak of a nose, a kind, comical face that Tim saw nearly every day, as the man would sit by himself in the depot reading the newspaper. He was obviously not a bum. He was clean and had fresh clothes every day, and Tim had seen him coming from the laundry with his blue-wrapped package of washed and folded things more than once. He might have been a remittance man, like so many. Somebody who was more or less being paid to stay away from home, or someone who had an income, but one so small it left him with free time but nothing to do. Tim had been seeing them for years; they were kind of sad, hanging around, got it made, but bored much of the time, and in this guy's case, too shy to make friends easily, and too homely to count himself in with the girls.

Patty must have made the overtures, because Flapears didn't seem the type. One day there they were, just the two of them, sitting in the window eating sandwiches and soup. Flapears did the paying, Flapears did the busing afterward, and Flapears held the back door open for her to precede him out onto the square. Tim, looking through the glass door from behind the counter, could see him grinning down at her, his hands in his hip pockets. She gave him a little hug and walked off. Tim also saw the quick look of pain on Flapears' face, then confusion. He turned and walked away, his hands still in his hip pickets, his ears catching the breeze.

More than once Tim saw them together outside or inside, and Flapears always seemed to be buying her something to eat. Then one day while he was sitting there reading his paper in came Patty with another guy, who bought her coffee and a piece of wreath cake. They sat right next to Flapears, but Patty paid him no attention. Aside from turning a bright red for a few moments, he seemed not to notice her.

But Tim worried about Patty. They had never caught whoever had murdered and cut up poor Barry Latimer, and there were other killers out there in the world, lots of them. Murdering young girls seemed almost fashionable these days. That wasn't the only reason he worried; he was a regular worrywart, as his father might have said.

One day as he was coming to work she was outside the back door bent over the garbage can throwing up. Tim wanted to turn away but instead he came up to her and asked, "Are you all right?"

Without turning she said, "Yes, thank you." Tim went inside to get her some paper towels but when he came back out she was gone. He told Fahima about her and admitted that Patty worried him.

"Don't worry about that one," Fahima said. "She is hard person."

"Yeah, maybe so," he said.

Another day he saw that guy in the green shirt and pants watching her, the guy he disliked so much without being able to say why.

Dick was his name. Perfect name for him, Dickhead, Dickface, Dickbrains. He was over standing in the shade of the big fir tree on the edge of the square, Patty was near the depot on the bench in the sun by herself. Actually, you couldn't be sure Dick was staring at her, but Tim was certain of it anyway, and it made him unreasonably angry, especially since it was none of his business.

Tim and everybody else who worked there also noticed that Four Eyes was interested in her, and that was kind of funny, kind of touching. Four Eyes was a nut, but a harmless sort of nut, and once you got used to him, not much of a problem. If he interrupted your conversation with his palaver about sending all the atom bombs to Mars you could say, "We're having a private conversation," or something and Four Eyes would leave you alone with an apology and a smile.

Fahima had nailed him once. Tim didn't know what to think about it. Four Eyes had been getting his refill at the counter and was telling Fahima that the world would be a better place without weapons. She had smiled and nodded and kept her eyes downcast as was her way, but Four Eyes wanted more, and said, "Don't you agree? Huh?"

"No," she said. She stopped what she was doing and looked at him calmly. There were no other customers in line. Tim was in the kitchen slicing onions.

"No?" said Four Eyes with a look of surprise on his face. "Why not?"

"With no weapons," she said, "Strong people would bully weak people."

"What?" he said. He looked stunned for a moment. He went to sit down and think about it. Soon he was smiling to himself, and later he came up to the counter when a whole line of people were crowded up there getting stuff. He said to Fahima in a loud voice, "No, you're probably wrong, it wouldn't be like that, people would cooperate . . ."

Fahima looked at Tim beside her and smiled sadly.

"You confused him," Tim said after Four Eyes had gone.

"Let him dream," she said.

But the next morning when there was a peaceful interlude, Four Eyes again accosted Fahima. "People would cooperate. Helping get rid of the weapons would change everybody."

"Look," Fahima said with concern in her eyes, "things are terrible now, all over world. We need our weapons. Children are dying." He just grinned at her with his head cocked, and she gave up. She smiled at him forgivingly, and waved away his offer to pay for his coffee. He thanked her, but put the money in the tip jar.

"He is nice man, but with mind of child," she said to Tim.

"I think he's got a case on Patty," Tim said.

"Too bad for him," was Fahima's comment. Women were sure tough.

ND then the Queen was gone. Some of the younger people who hung out around there said the boys in the white coats had come for her with butterfly nets and carted her off to the hospital; others said she had simply checked back in for her medication and had been kept in; she was suffering from exhaustion. She had been going without her medicine, according to the stories, because the King was taking it all, and she was suffering from malnutrition because the King was grabbing all her small allowance from the state.

What Four Eyes could see was that the King was spending a lot of time talking to Patty, who seemed fascinated by him—the only man she spent any time with who did not buy her food. Four Eyes was worried about her. He did not much like the King. He seemed like a wolf befriending rabbits. But Patty was no special friend to Four Eyes; she did not even seem to know he was alive. She had never really looked him in the eye, so she must have been a little surprised when he started sitting next to her out on the square, so that the King would be on one side of her and grinning Four Eyes on the other, nodding his head and looking foolish.

Once the King leaned forward, his hands hanging down between his legs, his greasy grey hair falling over his eyes, and said to Four Eyes, "Are you interested in our conversation?"

"Oh, no," he said. "Well, I'm sure it's very interesting, but I was just sitting here thinking about something else." He did not want to say that he wanted to be nearby in case Patty needed him. He did not know what she might need him for, but he wanted to be there anyway. The King really did worry him.

Patty did not care whether he hung around or not; just another man. The King interested her not for his money, he was a one-way street with money, but because he was so obviously what he was, with his mystical shuck and jive. All that crap about ancient Egypt covered a ruthless and cold-blooded man, and, she did not know why, such men attracted her. Probably something simple like her father, God damn him even in the memory, God damn him even though he was dead and in hell where he belonged, God damn him for dying before she could kill him herself. Not that she would have. He was like the King all right, unkillable, and if the stupid fuck hadn't gotten drunk and driven his car into a tree he'd still be around bugging Patty, turning everything around him into shit, as he so loved to do.

Four Eyes could hang around all he wanted. She knew he had money, he came in every morning and bought stuff, and she had heard, as most people had, that he was a Vietnam vet who had gone nuts over there and was on some kind of disability; he'd just go down to the Post Office once a month and get his check. Then he hid out somewhere. She had heard a couple of the guys at night talk about robbing Four Eyes but they hadn't done it yet. People around here were mostly bullshit anyway.

But finally she lost interest in the King. He was not like her father. She had let him fuck her in the backseat of his car and she lay there smelling all kinds of fetid shit while he fucked her and grunted in her ear, but she didn't get off and finally he just stopped fucking her without coming and pulled out, so he wasn't even much of a man. No money, no chops, fuck'im.

Patty measured all men against her father, and all women against her stupid fucking helpless mother. Mom taught Dad how to do it; she was the original Mrs. Punching Bag, that's probably how they met, he must have slugged her and she said, "Oh, do it again!" And he sure liked to do it. Again and again.

Patty's father had been beating the shit out of her and fucking her since she could remember, and only being flattened out against an old oak tree stopped him. The dirty son of a bitch would go out and get drunk all day and then come home at night for the Brutality Festival. He had fucked her within sight or hearing of her mother so many times she had lost count, but what difference did it make. Mom never did anything about it. If she pissed and moaned at all he'd tell her he was going to kill her, kill them both, and then himself. He was a peach.

The hell of it was, she had gotten off on him. Ain't that a bitch? No man had ever turned her on the way Daddy did, the poorly miserable son of a bitch, may he rot in hell forever, he had her coming in her jeans on the way home from school thinking about him, dreading him, terrified of him, but going home because if she didn't he would kill her; oh, she believed it for years, right up until the time the cops came over and looking all shy and stubbing their feet in the rug and saying he was dead, killed in a one-car wreck, and Mom blurting, "Oh, thank God!" making the cop look real surprised, young cop, raw face, lots of acne as a kid, she would have fucked him then and there, just to blow his mind, but she did not think of it. She had been, instead, thinking about her Dad. She even wasted a couple tears on the bastard, can you imagine?

She could never get over the contradiction; she hated and feared him more than anything on earth, yet he was the only one who could really make her jazz out behind fucking. Early training, maybe. She couldn't have been six when he started his little games, eating her baby pussy and fucking her in the ass. A real sophisticate, her dad. One of the best lawyers around, before the booze and the secret home life fried his brains.

So men. She knew men. She knew things about men they didn't have a clue to. What they were really like. Even Four Eyes coming around acting like he was a high school boy and wanting to carry her books. Given the opportunity he would drop the pose and take what he wanted. Whatever the hell that might be. He'd probably never had a fuck in his life, to be honest about it. He had that virgin look. She had fucked a couple of virgins. They came fast and didn't know what the hell to do anyway.

So anyway now the King didn't come around so much with his meal ticket in the hospital, and when he did he would sit by himself and look like he was deep in thought. Yet still Four Eyes would hang around like he was building up his nerve to ask her for a date. Just to blow his mind and because she was feeling hot and pissed off, she turned to him and said, "Are you tryin' to fuck me?"

He just grinned and cocked his head and said nothing, like he didn't hear her. The next day, though, he offered to buy her a sand-which, which she accepted. Part One, The Big Seduction.

She wondered idly how much she could get out of him before he understood that she would never fuck him in a million years. Fuck-ing meant nothing to her, but she knew men went crazy over it. She could take it or leave it alone. It was just like sneezing anyway, as one chick had told her. She wondered what Four Eyes would say, what his line would be, when finally he cut the shit and made his pass. Probably something real high school, like, "Oh, God, I love you!"

Patty had to laugh.

THE race began at the town square, ran up over the top of the mountain, and then down the rolling hills to the sea. Thousands of people came from everywhere to compete, and the owners of the depot decided that this year there were profits to be made by selling the amateur runners fruit juice or soft drinks in bottles. So, on this particular morning, Tim asked Fahima to come in and man a table with him outside the arches, on the square.

Tim griped to his wife but actually his heart was light and happy at the thought of spending the day—another hot one, but who cared?—with Fahima, and not in the madhouse he knew the depot would be, but out in the summer air. He swore to himself that this day he would not be manager at all, he would just be a happy-go-lucky employee, with nothing to do but hand out bottles and take in money. And be with Fahima.

When he got there Fahima had already set out the card table and chairs for them both, and was carrying out one of the washtubs full of ice. Her hair was pulled back severely, but one strand as usual had managed to get loose and hung down over her eyes. "You are late!" she said to Tim happily.

"Yes," he said happily. "Are you going to fire me?"

"Oh, no, I would not do such a thing," she said.

"But I'd better get right to work!" he said, and pretty soon all the tubs were in place, the hastily scrawled signs, "FRESH ORANGE JUICE ONE DOLLAR," "APPLE JUICE SIXTY CENTS," in place, Tim and Fahima at the new stand, sitting beside each other happily waiting for the crowd.

They did not have to wait long. Usually on Saturday morning at this hour there would only be a few regulars in the depot or on the square, but now hundreds of men, women, and young people were crowding the square and the street, dressed in running outfits, most of them standing around talking to one another, but many warming up, running in little circles, stretching muscles, or just wandering around in a hungover daze, wondering what the hell they were doing there. After a while Tim told Fahima he could see a cloud of adrenaline hanging over the square, and she laughed. "No, it is sweat," she said, and Tim almost fell off his chair.

Funny, the orange and other fruit jucies, the soda pop, and the things offered inside by the depot did not sell very well that morning. "Maybe," Tim said with a wry smile, "they don't want to fill up on acids before running on an otherwise empty stomach."

"I think you are right," Fahima said. "We are wasting our time."

"I'm happy," Tim said. "We can just sit here in the sunshine and collect wages. I don't give a hoot." And he *was* happy, his chest filled with expectancy. Everything delighted him. The thousands of runners crowding the square in their bright and mostly new running outfits, the clear hard blue of the sky, promising a brilliant hot day; and especially Fahima, sitting next to him in her red apron, pale yellow sweatshirt and tight jeans. Especially Fahima. He could not get over it; he was feeling almost dizzy with happiness. He tried to calm himself down. He told jokes at the expense of the runners. She laughed beautifully, and he told more jokes and she laughed some more, but nothing could cut the feeling, the incredible hopefulness that he could not explain.

"Oh Tim" she said. "We should do this every day. I would much rather sit here than work in kitchen."

"Any day," he said. "We could get one of those big beach umbrellas for when the sun gets too hot."

"Oh. I love the sun," she said, lifting her face to the light, closing her eyes.

Tim wanted to kiss her while her eyes were shut. A wave of emotion passed through him.

"How much is this orange juice?" a man asked. The man looked mean, overcivilized. His hair was cut too close and his running clothes were too new. "A dollar a cup," Tim said, indicating the stack of plastic coffee cups they were selling the juice in.

"My God, that's highway robbery," the man said.

"I'd have to agree with you," Tim said.

"How come it's so expensive?" the idiot insisted. Fahima looked at Tim expectantly. What was this spirit of deviltry between them this morning?

"I think it's the orange pickers," Tim said seriously. "Those goddam spicks want some kind of decent wage, or some shit like that."

The man went away and Fahima laughed immoderately. Tim was slightly flushed from his remark, which had been totally uncharacteristic of him. But he felt wonderful, more wonderful than he had ever felt. *Oh oh,* he thought. *Oh, holy shit. What's going on here?*

He knew; he just wouldn't admit it to himself. The morning moved forward, business was terrible, and finally the moment came when with a great shout, thousands of runners ran off up the street to the redwoods, into the forest, and up the side of the mountain. On the square, in the street, and inside the depot, were left the support people, the husbands, wives, and friends of the runners, who would relax, have coffee, smoke cigarettes, and then leisurely drive over the mountain and pick up their runners at the finish line. Then gradually they had all gone, and things were back to normal, the few regulars looking dazed and a little silly in their ordinary clothes.

Tim excused himself and went into the toilet, which had been too busy up to now. As he was washing his hands he looked at himself in the mirror, and saw a new man. Why? Who was this new man?

"I don't believe it," he said aloud, and then, "Oh, yeah? You don't believe it? Well, it's true!"

What's true?

He stared at himself, his hands under the cold running water. *You love her.*

"No," he said aloud, but it was hopeless. With a rising sense of joy, a bubbling of laughter starting deep in his soul, he banged out of the toilet, banged out of the depot, and found Hassan standing there with his hand on his wife's shoulder.

Tim should have deflated like a blown-out tire, but he did not. Hassan, good old Hassan, Handsome Hassie, who would have looked perfect standing in the doorway of a cut-rate jewelry store, a toothpick in the corner of his mouth. Hassan the husband. And Tim did not give a damn. Now that he had admitted it to himself, everything was different. He was excited, as excited as he had ever been, because *this, this* was *wrong*! No question about it.

And Tim did not give a fuck.

"Hello, Hassie!" he said cheerfully. He *liked* Hassie. Too bad. She didn't love him anyway.

"He is going to ocean," Fahima said to Tim, as if to tell him Hassie wouldn't be there long to bother their day together. "Going swimming."

"I want to watch the crazy people come running over mountain," Hassan said with his crooked grin. "Storing up memories of America," he said.

Tim felt his face go white and his stomach give a lurch. She was going back to Iran, in just weeks! Tim felt twelve years old. One moment in ecstacy, then the pit of despair. He had just admitted that, dirty bastard that he was, he loved her. Loved her, admit it, as he had never loved either of his wives.

"Go on to the beach," Fahima said to her husband in Farsi. "We're having a good time here. Tim is like a puppy today."

"I wish you could come with me," Hassan said.

"Another time," she said. "Go on now, so you can be back in time to pick me up."   cop. 1

"Are you sure you wouldn't rather go somewhere with your boss?" he asked, but not seriously. Tim watched them with an uncomprehending smile. What a nice guy, Hassie thought, not for the first time. He knew he could trust Tim.

"You never know what I'll find at the beach," he said to his wife. "Maybe I won't come back at all. You will have to go back to Persia by yourself."

"Good-bye, I am selling orange juice for a dollar a cup," she said to him with a sly smile.

"Good-bye all," Hassie said in English, and with a wave he left. Fahima and Tim looked at each other happily. Their lovely day would continue.

BUSINESS outside had dwindled down to near nothing, and Tim began to realize with some embarrassment that even though this fiasco had been the owners' idea, he had gone ahead and put himself and Fahima out here for full shifts. Had he done it simply to be with Fahima? He did not know, and did not care. But this was stupid; he would have to let her go. There was just nothing to do. And he should get home himself. There was a lot of crap to be done around the house. Husband crap. Dagwood doings. Shit.

"Excuse me?"

It was Four Eyes, peering down at them as they sat in the hot sunlight.

"I wonder if you've seen Patty this morning? With all the people around it's been a little confusing."

"I have not seen her," Fahima said to him gently. Tim noticed her tone; it was as if she were talking to a child.

"Me neither," Tim said as if talking to a man. "But we've been pretty busy." Ha ha.

Four Eyes moved off across the square and they watched him. "He's worried about her," Tim said.

"So are you," Fahima said. "But you don't have to worry about that one. She can take care of herself."

"I guess if anybody can," he said. "Well, I don't think we're doing much good out here. Maybe we'd better call it a day. Do you mind getting off early?"

"I will spend afternoon by myself," she said, and yawned, stretching her arms over her head, making Tim dizzy with desire. Yes, he had to admit that. Like admitting it was a little breezy in a typhoon. She laughed openly at the look on his face, and he knew the game was up. She knew he loved her.

"I love you," he said. No, he didn't. He only wanted to. He was not fool enough to. Well, what? Why not? She wouldn't laugh at him. She would only feel sorry for him.

Would she go to bed with him?

None of your business. Forget that. Shut up.

"I think I'll play hookey, too. I got a lot of stuff to do at home, but the hell with it. I feel like just lying in the sun somewhere."

"Oh!" she said with excitement. "Let's do it! Do you know a good place?"

He could not believe his luck. Either she was so innocent that she did not recognize the situation, or she was willing to go along with it. Oh, it was really nothing, a couple of friends spending some time together. That was all.

"We could have a picnic lunch, if you feel like it," Tim said.

"Oh, yes, a picnic lunch would be nice. We could go to park."

"I'll go buy some wine if you'll put us up some lunch," he said. "I think we've earned it."

He bought cold white wine at the liquor store and went back to the depot to wait for her while she fixed their lunch behind the counter, chattering with the other workers. Tim stayed outside so as not to crowd them. He had decided not to tell her he loved her. It would wreck everything. Yet he could not get over the idea that she loved him, too, or none of this would have come to a head. The suppressed excitement made him jittery, and he wished she would finish with the goddamn lunch so they could get out of there and be alone together. It seemed to take forever. They were chattering and laughing back there to beat the band, and he wanted to yell at them to shut up, but of course he did not.

And then she came out, carrying the sack of food, her face eager and smiling, and he all but fell to the floor kicking and screaming with love. "I'm sorry it took so long," she said.

"The time flew by," he said, and held the door open for her.

As he was coming out, she turned to him and they bumped. He thought he would go out of his mind with her closeness. "Oh, do you have opener for wine?" she asked. So practical.

"I have my Swiss Army knife," he said proudly, and they walked up the street together, bumping from time to time.

The park began only a short distance away, and soon they were under the delicious shade of the redwoods, awestruck as always by the remarkable cathedral light, where the sunshine filtered down through the foliage, this rich multicolored light sharply defined against the deep velvet darkness. The ground was soft with its thickness of decaying redwood foliage, and as they walked silently, Tim felt her take his hand. Her hand was warm and dry and soft against his. If he had not already been desperately in love, he would have been now.

There were some people wandering around in the park, and little children over by the sandbox and playground equipment, so they kept walking along the streambank, up past the back of the library, and then along a path where some scrub trees grew along the bank, and then they broke out into the open, a redwood grove lit like a church, with a picnic bench, an old outdoor wood cookstove, and a standpipe with a brightly worn brass faucet.

"Here is our place," said Fahima. "Oh, I am hungry now!"

"Did you bring paper cups for us?"

"Of course. We could not drink from bottle. We would look like winos."

He laughed. The wine opened and poured into their Styrofoam coffee cups, Tim raised his in a salute, and so did Fahima. "To us," he wanted to say, like any movie lover, but instead he said, "To you."

"But I cannot drink to that," she said. "To you, also."

They drank together, eyes locked, and Tim was absolutely certain she loved him. But not certain enough to say anything.

As they ate they talked quietly about depot matters. The wine they sipped had no effect on Tim, but Fahima grew silly, and her large dark eyes grew even larger and, if possible, more beautiful. Tim began having that high-school-boy anxiety about making a pass. Should he, or shouldn't he? Would he spoil the magic? Either way? What, oh what, was he to do? It was really very comical.

And then: "Oh, Teem, I must kiss you, I am so happy!" She kissed him. Both were sitting on the picnic table, their feet on the bench, lunch finished, the wine half gone, Tim thinking wildly about asking her to go to the storeroom with him. He could just hear himself: "Let's go to the storeroom and make love on the supplies!"

But the one kiss was all. The afternoon moved to a close, and they walked slowly back, back to the depot and their lives. Hassie the Handsome was waiting for them, talking to Edna, the big blonde who had just come on shift. Fahima spoke to him rapidly in Persian and the day was over for Tim. He spoke to the workers, checked the tape, thanked Fahima, made a joke with Hassie, and went numbly out to his car to head for home. He wondered how in the name of God he was going to face Claire, his wife.

H E was not really worried about her; he knew she could take care of herself. But she was too trusting. She spent time with men who looked to Four Eyes very dangerous. But she had also spent time with Four Eyes, and he liked her. He bought things for her because she expected it, even though the money he spent cut sharply into his own strict budget. He did not ask of her that she talk to him, go for walks with him, listen to him. But she did.

Once they had gone for a long walk on the mountain together, and he remembered that as the best time. He had talked about everything under the sun. He had told her the names of plants, flowers, birds, insects, rocks, different types of clouds, the animals that lived up there, all the random knowledge he had picked up over the years of wandering, the names and identifications that he was quick to tell her really meant nothing.

"It's not the name, it's the animal," he said.

"It's awful goddamn hot up here," she said.

"Oh, we could sit in the shade for a while if you're hot," and took her over to a shady rock.

"This rock is hard," she said. They sat looking at the view, the tops of redwoods below them, the town, the marsh, everything.

"This is granite," he said. "Quartz, mica, and feldspar."

"You must of learned all this crap in the Boy Scouts, huh?"

"Oh, I was never a Boy Scout," he said. "I was alone a lot and I read a lot. It doesn't mean anything, just something to talk about when you're walking along. I love to walk."

"Me, too," she said.

"This old mountain is covered with trails," he said. "We could walk and walk and never be in the same place twice, even on a small mountain like this. When the rains come I could show you all the different mushrooms that must grow up here."

"Any kind to eat? I thought they were all poison."

"There's plenty to eat and plenty of poison ones," he said. "Do you like mushrooms?"

"No," she said.

"Not even mushroom soup?" he joked, but she did not seem to know he was joking. She looked at him without expression and said, "I don't like soup."

"Oh," he said, "I saw you eating soup at the depot, they have good soup, I eat it myself all the time."

"Can we get the hell out of here? I think the bastard's probably gone by now."

She got down off the rock and so did he. "Who are you talking about?" he asked.

"This creep," Patty said. She grinned her boyish grin and held out her hand to Four Eyes. He took it, feeling himself blush, but as they began to walk down the trail she let his hand go. That was all right, too; his hand was beginning to sweat. Patty went on: "Yeah, this guy's been bothering me, and I saw him drive up and look for a parking place, so when you said let's go . . ." She shrugged, and kicked at a rock.

When they got back down to the depot he did not want to lose her company, so he offered to buy her a sandwich. His money was running out, but she needed to eat, too. And if he did not buy her food, he knew she would get somebody else to, and he did not like to think of what might be going on. She had no respect for herself. That worried him.

She ate her sandwich while he watched. It was getting late, and soon it would be night. He did not know where she spent her nights.

He did not want to ask, and she had not said. He was afraid she was sleeping with different men, just to get in out of doors. He did not blame her, but he wished she wouldn't. He had to admit he was fond of her.

"I have to go," she said at last. She wiped her mouth. "Thank you for the food." And she was gone, no mention of the hours together that day, hours that Four Eyes cherished. He lay in his bedroll in the salt marsh later that night thinking about her and how he had babbled all day long. At least he had not babbled about his plan. He believed in himself and in his plan, but he did not expect her to believe. She had become too hard over the years. He could tell. But even her very hardness appealed to him.

Now, on the evening of the big race over the mountain, he hung around. The sun was dropping behind the redwoods throwing cool shadows over the square. Even if he found her she would leave him. But it pained him to think so. He wished he could talk her into spending the nights with him in the marsh. She would be safe and warm, he would see to that. And they could talk in the darkness. But he was afraid to even bring it up, for fear she would laugh at him. He was no lover, he knew that, but for her he would try.

But he could not even find her. He had not made friends with anybody else on the square, and so there was no one to sit with or talk to. He had explained his plan to nearly everybody around there by now, anyway. They laughed at him or agreed with him, and that was that. He could see one bunch of guys sitting near him passing a bottle back and forth. The drinking had started early that day, maybe because of all the runners that morning, and the guys were pretty drunk by now. Four Eyes had learned long ago to be wary of drinking men. Sometimes they forgot themselves and would get nasty. The best thing to do was get away. Four Eyes himself did not like to drink. There was another group of young guys standing around the back of an old pickup truck, with their big dogs in the back of the truck.

These were pretty bad guys, he knew, always shouting at people or getting into fights. The police came to break things up almost every night, he had heard. Now there was a quick dogfight, yelling and whooping, everybody having a good time. He sat on the bricks with his back against the depot and watched.

Sherman, too, was drunk. Had been drunk. And would get drunker. This had been a red-letter day for Sherman. He had nailed several of those motherfuckers for money, and he was rich beyond his wildest dreams. This was going to be a good cheerful evening, as far as Sherman was concerned. That is, until he saw the gloomy puss of old Four Eyes, sittin' there lookin' like the asshole he was.

"Hey, asshole," Sherman said. He stood over Four Eyes, who peered up grinning.

"Hello," he said with his idiot grin.

"Hello fuck you," Sherman said. "Are you just going to sit there, or are you going to join me in a drink?"

"Oh, no thank you," Four Eyes said, and got to his feet, lookin' like a cornered sheep or somethin'.

"Well, I offer you a free drink and you turn me down. What kind of shit is that? I ask you."

"Fuck off," said Patty to the rescue. Here she was, li'l bitch, wouldn't even give Sherman the time of fuckin' day. Now what?

"Who the fuck are you?" Sherman asked her.

"Just fuck off," she said, and took Four Eyes' arm.

PATTY really liked the guy, that was the funny part. She couldn't remember when she had actually liked anybody. If ever.

"Come on," she said, tugging on his arm, "let's sit over here and talk a minute."

"All right," he said. "Yes, I'd like to talk. I was looking for you. Oh, not really looking, just wondering where you were. Have you had anything to eat?"

He was like a God damn mother hen sometimes. "Yes, I ate," she said. They sat down on the low concrete retainer around the fir tree. "You got to look out for guys like that Sherman," she said. "He gets pretty drunk, and then he's really unpredictable."

"I know," Four Eyes said. He seemed pretty happy. They just sat there for a few minutes without talking. It was nice.

But it didn't last long. This guy she had been looking for stuck his head out of the depot, saw her, and went back inside. "Okay," she said, getting up. "That's it for me." He got up too, looking a little confused.

She touched his arm. "Hey, you gonna be all right? You don't come around at night much. It's different. Maybe you better go home now. You got someplace to go?"

"Oh, yes. You could come with me. There's room for two," he said anxiously. He was peering down at her, and she realized that at last he was making his move. The move she thought he was never going to make. Or would be corny.

"You'd be safe with me," he said. Nobody had ever said that to her.

It was almost tempting, the thought of being safe. But no. She was pretty low-down, she knew, but not that low-down.

"I'll see you tomorrow," she said. "You can buy me a corn muffin with butter."

He smiled. He had a really nice smile, once you got through the idiot grin aspect of it.

The guy inside the depot was money in the bank. She figured he was worth at least a hundred, a dollar for every pound he was overweight. He had been hinting around, and now it was time to collect. Commuter type. Had a big station wagon, a sports car, big house in the shadows, wife, kids, dog, the works. Sleazing around the depot looking for pussy, while he's supposed to be out running. Nice new running suit, never even broke into a sweat in it. What a fucking hog. She knew how to handle that type. She wouldn't even pull off her panties for him. A quick blowjob if he really played his cards right. She knew how to do it so the bastard would come in about three seconds. He'd have it and he wouldn't. Heh heh.

She set her face cold as she pushed open the glass back door to the depot.

Four Eyes watched her with a sinking heart. He knew she was going to meet some man; he only hoped she knew what she was doing. Well, it was time to walk down to the marsh, the end of another day. But he did not want to move. If he stayed, maybe she would come back. Maybe she would change her mind and come with him. He did not know. He just sat there, not wanting to move. Disturbed. Troubled. He did not know why he should be particularly troubled tonight.

After a while he saw Patty come out of the depot with a man, a heavy-looking man. They got into a little red car and drove away. Four eyes sighed. Maybe he should go in and have a last cup of coffee and then go down to the marsh. He got up and started across the square, but with a surprising jolt he was knocked flying by something, somebody. He felt the bricks harsh against his cheek and felt his glasses go flying. "Oof!" he heard somebody else say. "Sombitch!"

Four Eyes felt a sharp pain in his left hand. He had skinned his palm and the hurt was increasing. He could see a white blur, a tee shirt, with a big white face above it. "Sombitch, you asshole!" said the boy.

"Hey, what the fuck!" yelled somebody else.

Four Eyes did not say anything about his glasses. He did not want to draw attention to them. But he felt around for them, still on his knees, as the group of boys surrounded him.

"Hey, it's the creep," one of them said.

"Yeah, fuckin' Four Eyes," said somebody else.

"Leave the fucker alone," said a voice.

"Kick his ass!"

"Hey, you got any money, man?"

"Christ Almighty he's a dirty son of a bitch, ain't he? He could use a God damn bath!"

Four Eyes got to his feet, forgetting about his glasses. This was a tense situation. He did not want to provoke them. He could smell they had been drinking beer. He met no one's eyes, and tried to sidle away from them, but somebody grabbed him and then somebody else and he found himself being carried along into the shadows over where the cars were parked. He felt himself bumped against a car, hands searching his clothes, a fist hitting him. He did not try to speak to them; he knew it would only make things worse.

They found his straight razor, and with yells of glee they decided his hippie hair had to go, and so, holding him down, they shaved his head with the naked razor. It hurt a lot, but he did not cry out.

"Awright, you stupid bastards," came a deep rumbling voice. "Lay off before I have to knife a couple you fuckers."

"Back off, Sherman," said an uncertain young voice.

"Back off you fuckin' *shit!*" Sherman roared. "You wanna DIE?"

Pretty soon they were gone. Four Eyes got to his feet and looked at Sherman, a blur leaning against a car. "Thank you," he said.

"You wanna drink?" Sherman asked in his gravelly voice.

"No, thank you. I'll get some water."

"Those jive fuckers," Sherman said. "I wasn't rescuin' you, like that chick. I was just kickin' some ass."

"I understand," said Four Eyes. As he made his way across the square, the air cold on his shaven head, a small man came up to him and handed him his glasses.

"Oh, thank you," Four Eyes said, and put them on. But the little man had gone back to his friends, who were all sitting there passing a bottle.

He looked at himself in the depot men's room mirror. They had done a bad job, but there was not much blood, and what there was washed away, leaving a couple of red lines on his blue-white scalp. There were little jagged lines of stubble, too, where they had missed. His razor was gone. He wondered how he would shave in the morning. He wondered what Patty would think. He thought about the boys who had done this. They were only boys, but he wished they hadn't done it.

Dɪᴄᴋ did not wear green at night; those were his work clothes, and he had six sets of green shirts and pants, one for each workday. Tonight he was dressed in designer jeans in spite of his meaty upper legs, and a flowered cowboy shirt with snap buttons that made him sweat because the fabric was some kind of plastic instead of cotton. He had the sleeves rolled up past his elbows. He knew he had good-looking arms, all muscled and tan. He was tan right up to the biceps, but his body was white. Dick did not go out sunbathing or to the beach or anything. In fact, he led a pretty dull life, all in all.

He sat in his dark FIX-M-UP van watching the little red MG tool out of the parking lot and turn left, toward the freeway. He could start his engine now, and follow, or not. He felt the trickle of excitement, bright as blood, as he reached forward and turned the key. *Tonight.* This one would be different. Bitch Barry had been a totally out of control thing. He had just gone nuts, he had to admit to himself.

Keeping his distance he followed the little sports car down as far as the freeway, where it turned off onto the frontage road. Past the building supply, where he was in and out all week long, the motel, the Chinese restaurant, the exercise place with all the fantastic chicks, and the parking lot in front of the swing bar where Dick had been eighty-six for months, over some minor little fuss when he made a humorous remark and some guy got hot about it. Well, he had no plans for going inside. He sat at the far end of the lot and watched fat boy and Patty walk into the place. She was dressed wrong for this kind of dump, but nobody cared about how the chicks dressed, just the guys.

Waiting was good. He was pretty excited. He didn't really know if this was going to be the night or not, but he knew he was ready. He had been building up for days, watching her, getting more and more pissed off at the way she hung around with those bums on the square, especially that creep Four Eyes. Here Dick says hello to her once and she looks at him like the dog just shit on her foot, and fucking Four Eyes walks up and she talks to him, goes for fucking walks with him, and for all Dick knew, fucked him inside and out. A real pissoff.

Dick knew all about Four Eyes. He had seen him coming up out of the salt marsh a couple of times. He knew the clump of trees where the creep stashed his goods and slept at night. He had never seen Patty down that way, but you never knew with a little bitch like that.

While he waited he entertained himself with memories of Barry Latimer, whom he had killed good, even though he had gone ape-shit at the time. He had tried to pretend to forget, but there were little things all over that finally convinced him his imaginings and dreams were really memories, his own memories, and the excitement had been real.

Nothing like it. Absolutely nothing. Had been holding it in for years, all his life, holding it in until he was about to bust, and then *did* bust, all over that bitch. Just nuts. Blood all over himself, one each suit of greens finished, pair of shoes, socks, shorts. Him nuts with it all, coming and going from his truck about ten times, then days of cleaning the van and himself, still finding patches of blood on himself for a week. He could not believe how dumb the cops were, or how lucky he had been to get away with it, all unplanned, just the way she had looked at him with that don't-hold-your-breath look, and then *wham*. Nuts.

But not this time. This time he meant to get the full fun of it. There would be sex this time, not just craziness. He would have sex the way he wanted it. She would just have to put up with it. Oh, he knew he disgusted women, although he did not know why. The really beautiful ones wouldn't even look at him. This one looked at him. Like he was a hunk of shit. Well, that was just fine. He would stuff his pecker up her ass and see how she looked. He would slice off her tits and we'd see what we would see.

But he stopped that kind of thought. No use spoiling things in advance; he could get thinking like this and come in his pants and wreck everything. No, there was no real chance of that. He had built up his nerve, and here he was. And the beautiful part; if things weren't just perfect, he didn't have to make his move at all. Only if things were perfect.

Finally they came out of the place, after about an hour. Dick was really mad, but he kept it in and followed at a safe distance. They didn't go far, just as far as the motel, and then Dick got really pissed off. Wasn't she ever going to leave this bastard? He sat out in his van across the road from the motel entrance, the feeling dying in him, the feeling that tonight would be the night, when she came out the entryway on foot, just suddenly like that, after only about ten or fifteen minutes in the cabin. Then the guy came running out in his pants but no shirt. She started walking down the road and the guy shook his fist and yelled, "Whore!" and Dick started his engine.

It was so easy. As he approached her she turned and stuck out her thumb. He pulled up and opened his passenger door.

"Hop in," he said.

"Oh, it's you."

"Aw, get in, I won't hurt you."

She got in. He felt a delicious sense of power. Everything was just fine, everything was going to be perfect. The excitement was wonderful, incredible, worth it, worth anything.

Outwardly he was calm and in control, calmer than usual, almost relaxed. As they drove down the frontage road toward the freeway entrance he thought about the one big problem he had in front of him. Once he got the van into his garage and the garage door shut everything would be fine; he could rassle her down into the basement where everything was waiting. But before that he had to get control of her, to keep her from jumping out of the van the minute she knew. That was the tricky moment; he had gone over it in his mind a thousand times with a thousand different imaginary girls.

Now it was real. He had no gun or handcuffs or chloroform, he had not rigged the lock on the passenger side so that it wouldn't work—he would just have to rely on brute strength, hit her one on the chops, rassle her into the back, tie her up, and gag her. Right here, at the freeway entrance. Now. *Now*

No. They moved out onto the freeway, and she said without looking at him, "I wanna go back to the square."

"Why? You got somethin' to do? Somewhere to go?"

"I got somewhere to go," she said.

"I'll take you right to the depot," he said. The next stopsign after we get off the freeway. That would be the place. Might as well be friendly. "You really took that guy for a ride, huh?"

"What guy?"

"You know, the guy who was yellin' at you."

"He musta been drunk," she said.

"You're not very friendly," he said.

"Yeah, I guess not," she said. He looked over at her. She was scrooched down in the seat. If he backhanded her in the face with his right hand she'd at least be stunned enough for him to rassle her into the back. She hadn't fastened the seat belt.

"Somethin's screwed up, here," he said with deepening excitement. He drove around the tight curve of the freeway exit, a set of lights behind him. Up the road a little was a wide spot next to some trees. "Gotta pull over a sec," he said. He pulled over and the car behind went past him.

"What's the matter?" she said.

"I think maybe somethin' in the fuel line," he said, and pulled on the handbrake.

"I'll get out here," she said quickly.

Making a high-pitched sound he swung at her. The bitch ducked and his fist grazed the top of her head. It was all out in the open now.

"God damn whore!" he said tightly and made a grab for her. But from the moment the van stopped Patty had been on guard, and now her blood was up. He was big and powerful and fast and desperate, but she was not frightened. She felt a mind-emptying anger, and she fought back like a mad animal. He grabbed at her to get her in a bear hug and somehow move her into the back of the van, but she was strong, much stronger than she had any right to be, and he could not get his hands on her. He was yelling and she was silent. They fought clumsily, and he cut one of his knuckles on the door, cursing angrily at her and slapping at her head. She tried to turn and get the door open, but he pulled her back around and got his hand on her neck. He was angry, too, much angrier than she was, his own animal rage blinding him to what was happening. He shook her as a dog might shake a bird. It was some time before he realized that she had gone limp. Dumbly he noticed the lights of cars going past.

In the flashing lights he could see that her eyes were open, even though she did not move. Her head lay at an odd angle, and as the red rage subsided, he knew he had killed her. Broken her neck.

"Oh, for God's sake," he said in a throaty voice. He started the van and drove for a while. He drove past the depot and up into the redwoods, breaking out on the road leading to the top of the mountain. He drove around not thinking, not knowing what to do next, for almost an hour.

She had spoiled everything. She was dead. That was not what he wanted, not yet. He had wanted to tie her up, let her know what was happening to her, make her know it was *him*, that he had the power of life and death over her, and he was the one who was going to kill her, he would be the one who—oh, hell. It was all over. The wonderful feeling had gone away, and he did not know how he could get it back. Meanwhile, he was stuck with the body. What a disappointment. This bitch was even more of a disappointment than Bitch Barry had been. Dead.

Eventually he drove home, to his little cottage with attached garage. In he drove, closing the door with his remote control. He sat there with the lights out for a few moments, trying to gather strength. He was so tired. This shit really took it out of you. But, he thought after a while, maybe there's still some fun to be had. Yes. Of course. Why stop now? He had the bitch, might as well.

He took the body down into his full basement, draped over his shoulder in the approved fireman's grip. The basement, lit by its four overhead naked bulbs, looked neat as a pin as usual. The workbench you could eat off of, every tool on the pegboard was inside its painted outline, the tablesaw was cool under its cover; everything was neat and clean and orderly; even the Playboy Playmates in a row down one wall were all neatly tacked up and the creases ironed out of them. "Hello, girls," he said, as he dumped Patty's body on the workbench. Fucking eyes were still open.

He had gotten things ready before. The enamel-topped table from the kitchen was down here, with a sheet of heavy-duty plastic covering it. Put the body over there. My God, she was stiffening up already, and would not lie out quite flat. Her legs would not cooperate. He had a hard time undressing her, but finally it was done, her clothing placed neatly folded into a shopping bag for later disposal. She lay nude on the plastic, not at all appealing anymore. God damn her bitch anyway, cunt, died too quick.

He looked at the big hook he had screwed into the overhead beam. He was gonna hang her from that by the hands. No point in it now. He went upstairs, slowly, dragging his feet, to pick out which of his knives he would use. He had daydreamed that this would be one of the good parts, but it wasn't. The knives he kept in the hall closet, locked, all eight hundred of them, neatly racked, the racks of cardboard hung like coats. He just took the first one that came to hand, an old butcher knife he had stolen from that wop restaurant down the freeway.

He went back downstairs and stripped off his clothes, feeling a growing sense of dread. He approached the body. Dead bitch. How could she have died like that? He almost wanted to cry. Wouldn't it ever be right? Why did they have to fight? Why did they hate him?

He cut off her head. It was no fun. There wasn't even that much blood. He had daydreamed about cutting off her head, wildly exciting daydreams. But the reality was a bore, and he didn't bother to do any more cutting. All the things he had planned to do were bitter in his mouth, now.

She had really taken all the fun out of it. The dirty whore.

FOUR Eyes went around saying that he had cut off his own hair and had done such a bad job because he had tried to do it without a mirror. But Tim and everybody else guessed that somebody had done it to him. He looked terrible, his scalp a blue-white, making his normal skin look sallow. Also, he was not his calm crazy old self, but seemed more nervous. He kept asking people if they had seen Patty, but nobody had.

Tim hoped she had gone away, but he felt sorry for Four Eyes. The old woman, Dorothy, told him all about the midnight haircutting. Sherman had told her about it. "Some pretty tough kids," she said. "They oughtta put 'em in the service or somethin', calm 'em down."

Tim remembered somebody somewhere, apropos of war, saying that there was no one meaner or crueller than a nineteen-year-old American boy. He shuddered with agreement just thinking about it, and remembering his own youth. Four Eyes must have come up to them with his nut plan for putting all the atomic bombs on a rocket ship for the moon, and they turned on him.

Tim was relieved when Four Eyes found a scarlet cap to wear, something somebody knitted for somebody's Christmas about a hundred years ago, from the look of it, a stocking cap with a small scarlet tassel on the end, and dark spots of maybe grease, where the cap had been left on somebody's garage floor. Where Four Eyes found it Tim did not know. But the guy looked less ridiculous, somehow, with the goddamn cap on.

But now he looked so lonely sitting around not even scavenging newspapers, just sitting there with a half a cup of coffee, waiting for

Patty to show up. Too bad, too bad. But Tim had a lot more on his mind than the loves and lives of the people on the square.

He had lain awake nearly all night after his picnic with Fahima, his wife's body next to him in the king-size bed, her breathing deep and regular, so that at least he did not have to worry about her being awake. She was so sensitive; often, if he was unable to sleep, she, too, would be awake. "Is there anything the matter?" she might ask, while his mind raced. But not this night. He was alone with his thoughts, and what thoughts.

Should he run away with Fahima? Ha ha. It had been wonderful, ecstatic, to allow himself to know that in spite of everything, he did love her. It was like puppy love, except that he was not a puppy anymore. At first he had not even been able to imagine her naked; now her nakedness filled his imagination; he lusted for her as passionately as any boy ever lusted for any girl.

Tim did not doubt that he could get her away from Hassan. He was ashamed at himself for thinking about breaking up somebody's marriage—ha, two marriages—so lightly, but in the face of his realization that not only did he love her, he had never really loved anybody else, what could he do? This was it, this was the real thing, and all his life he had been taught, told, made to believe, that no matter what else, you went after your true love. Even if it ended in tragedy, à la Romeo and Juliet.

"But soft, what light at yonder window breaks?"

Now, what the fuck does that mean? It means that for a kid, Romeo had quite a way with the old mother tongue. Tim wished he had the gift of gab, as Irish are supposed to. He didn't. The gift of putting his foot in his mouth was more like it. Oh, he could get her away from Hassan, because she didn't love him, as Tim never tired of telling himself. Poor Hassie, after a certain amount of personal agony, would be relieved to find that he did not, after all, have to accompany his firebrand wife back to certain death in Iran. He could stay in America and go into business, as God had intended.

DIAMOND RINGS $39.99 GUARANTEED GENUINE!!

But. And once again the dream collapsed, punctured by a but. But. He knew in his sinking heart that he could never pull Fahima away from her own intentions. She would go back there, to that ancient land riddled with poverty, ignorance, and death. Where, because she had tasted six years of American freedom, she would unknowingly give some petty official the wrong look or say the wrong thing, and away she would go, to jail, to torture, to death. It was unbearable to think of her blindfolded in front of a wall, or in the middle of a parking lot somewhere, being shot down, her magnificent arrogance untouched, but her magnificent body defiled by stupid bullets. Or worse, yes, worse, that beauty, that intelligence, that spirit, locked in a filthy cell to age and die. Oh, God, he couldn't stand thinking about it, he had to get out of bed and run into the bathroom sobbing in the middle of the night, hoping he hadn't awakened his wife.

No. Back in bed, calm but cold, he knew he could not get her to do that. To leave that. To not go. So there were, at best, a few weeks left in which to make her love him. And have an affair. And then say good-bye. Oh, God, why, why, why did he have to fall in love with a doomed woman? Why, God? Do you know this is why I left you, God? You never answer my questions, that's why.

It would be even better, he knew, not to have an affair (as if it were up to him!) and just keep his fucking mouth shut. But no. She would know. One look at him and the whole world would know, must already know, probably knew before he did. His face reddened hotly. His wife! Claire must already know. She was so damned sensitive to him! Damn her for being so sensitive!

The next day at work was a chore, and only the stories of Four

Eyes' walpurgisnacht distracted him from his task of trying to find
out if Fahima or anybody else around there suspected that he had
fallen for her. She was sweet to him, as usual, her eyes bright and
happy, but she spent most of the shift (when not busy) talking to the
old woman about her cat, and the old woman's cat, and cats in
general. Tim had never much cared for cats, being a dog man (sans
dog) but now he actively hated the little bastards. Fahima was
actually going to take her cat back to Iran.

"Don't they have cats there already?"

"Oh, yes. Famous. Persian cats, very expensive."

Tim said a nasty thing, regretting it almost immediately, but
Fahima did not seem to notice: "With all that hunger, you'd think
people would eat cats," he said. Cruelly.

"Oh, they kill them, burn them, I have seen little animals
hanged. Everything," she said. She was making soup, stirring the
big full kettle as she talked, sniffing, tasting, as he had taught her.
"Near my house is, what you call it, empty lot. When I walk past I
see terrible things boys do to little animals. It is not like here. If boys
see birds they do not admire. Right away they throw stones."

"That sounds terrible." Any bad word he could put in about Iran.

"They are uneducated," she said. She did not seem to know she
was the object of his sole and true love. He had to laugh. Him and
Four Eyes. Just a couple of lovestruck kids.

O N the last day of the worst heat wave anybody had seen around there, Valerie, who seemed unaffected by the extraordinary weather, at last finished his bed cover. He had kept it as clean as possible, considering one thing and another, but he would have it dry-cleaned before making his presentation. A certain retired Marine gunnery sergeant was going to be wonderfully surprised, or Valerie knew nothing of human nature. The bed cover was, if he said so himself, rather pretty. All crimson, green, and a rich brown, its pattern not really a pattern but an apparently random design that just luckily seemed to create its own rude harmony.

Valerie stood up with his work and held it up, his arms outstretched, to give it a shake to get rid of redwood twigs, needles, and dirt particles. Tim came out of the depot hot and red-faced, crossed the street, and stood looking at Valerie's handiwork, his head tilted critically to one side.

"Gee, that's really beautiful," he said to Valerie.

"You sound surprised," Valerie said tartly.

"I *am* surprised," Tim said with a nice grin.

"Well, thank you for the compliment, anyway," Valerie said. "I should wash it by hand, but I'm afraid to, for fear the shrinkage wouldn't come out even, you know, like a Navaho blanket. They hold water, you know. But I'll just get it dry-cleaned."

"I never saw anything like it," Tim admitted. "You ought to win a prize or something."

"Well, thank you very much," Valerie said, folding up his bed cover carefully.

"How about something from the depot, on the house?" Tim

asked. "A *latte,* pastry, sandwich? I'm afraid we don't have much to offer."

"I'd love a nice pastry," Valerie said.

Tim escorted him across the street, with his big workbag, sat him down at the big table in the middle of the dining room, and saw to it that he had a *caffe latte* and a piece of blueberry Danish pastry. With Valerie's permission, Tim held up the bed cover for everyone to see. Everyone was really impressed by its beauty and the high quality of the workmanship.

But it was Fahima who asked the question that was on everyone's mind: "Please, after police take you away last time, they don't bother you anymore. What happened?"

Valerie smiled proudly up at the beautiful Persian girl. "Oh, the judge gave me a suspended sentence. He was a nice man, just like that judge on television. He gave them quite a tongue-lashing, too. Told them not to harass me. He really made fun of the district attorney man. I guess that's why they don't bother me anymore."

Fahima laughed. "You made them ashamed, how wonderful!"

After a really very pleasant half hour, Valerie got up to leave. Everyone wanted to shake his hand.

"Well, I'm finished here now," he said, and went to catch his bus. Nobody around there ever saw him again.

Four Eyes had not been able to get interested in Valerie's workmanship. It was very beautiful, yes, but Four Eyes had too much on his mind to think about such things. Where was Patty? Had he said or done anything to drive her away? Had anybody else? Was she in trouble? Where did she spend her nights? He could not answer any of these questions, so they just rolled around and around in his mind, a deep anxiety constricting his heart.

Finally, when the hot sun had dropped behind the redwoods and the square cooled somewhat, Four Eyes reluctantly left, walking down the street that had originally been the railroad right-of-way. By the time he left the road and was on the bike path into the salt marsh, the sun had gone down completely and a fat roll of white-grey fog hung over the hills to the west. The breeze against his cheek was actually chilly. After the heat, it should have made him feel good, but it didn't. He was still worried about Patty, afraid that he had said or done something to drive her away.

At his campsite he pulled his things out of their hiding place under the tree. For supper he had four thick slices of salami and a peach. The peaches were just coming in, and they were delicious. Four Eyes did not like to build fires out here, because they would be too easy to spot. He swallowed his vitamin and mineral tablet dry, and then laid out his bedroll. It was dark now, and the wind blowing steadily chill, the fog blotting out the stars to the west. Eventually, as he lay there unable to sleep, the fog covered the whole night sky.

He fell asleep after a while. It had been a long day, full of anxiety. He awakened shortly before dawn. The sky was a cold steel grey. He lay quietly for a few minutes, and then the anxiety of the past few days reentered him, and he sat up. Looking around blankly, half-awake, he saw the paper bag not twenty feet from him, near the path through the marsh grass. Just a paper bag, somebody's lunch sack, except it had not been there the night before. The wind rattled it but did not move it. There was something heavy inside. Somebody had brought it here and left it.

Four Eyes was not at all prepared for what he found in the sack. It was Patty's head, stinking like stale hamburger. He dropped the bag and her head fell out.

"No," he said mildly. "Oh, no. No."

He was on his knees. Pain was crushing him. Disbelief was all he could feel, with her head lying right there in front of him. And then he cried, great bellowing sobs shaking his body as he kneeled in the wet grass, his arms at his sides. Through hot tears he saw the paper bag blow away, leaving its obscene contents for Four Eyes to deal with.

After a while, when thought returned, he could only believe that if he had been man enough, she would have come with him, stayed with him, and been safe. If only he had been more of a man.

With this thought bludgeoning his mind, he got to his feet and stumbled off down the path, leaving Patty's head where it lay. He did not know where he was going, or what he was doing. He was barefoot and had left all his things out. He walked along, looking toward the mountain, but the mountain was covered in fog.

TIM's absorption with himself and his own problems was interrupted by the appearance of Four Eyes that morning. Tim happened to have stepped out the back door for a moment to wipe his eyes and get a little relief from cutting up the big yellow onions, a task that was not his but had fallen to him more and more often when he was around—everybody hated it. Even the bread delivery man had complained. But people had to have their God damned onions.

Tim looked at the grey sky with some relief. The heat had been getting to him. This was more like it; the summer pattern of fog and mild sunshine was more to his taste. But here across the square came Four Eyes, bareheaded and barefoot, slogging along, the light reflecting off his glasses. Four Eyes had not shaved in days, and with his hair slowly growing back in he really looked a sight. He did not smile or even look at Tim as he walked past into the depot. He did not stop at the busing trays and squat down to riffle through the morning's newspapers. He did not get anything at the counter, but sat at a table by himself, looking out at nothing.

"Are you okay?" Tim asked him. But Four Eyes did not answer. Instead he stood up abruptly and went back out onto the square. Tim shrugged and went back into the kitchen, where there was work to be done. She was there, making soup.

"I think old Four Eyes is starting to peak," he said.

"What do you mean?"

"I think he's getting ready to flip," Tim said. But he could not seem to get Fahima to understand that going without shoes or shaving might be an indication of mental illness.

"At home many people like that," she said.

"Get a look at him, when you can," he said. "And tell me what you think."

So when Fahima had a moment she stepped out onto the square, wiping back a strand of hair from her forehead and breathing the sharp clean air. She was just in time to see the four police cars slide up from all directions, two of them bumping the curb and driving right up on the square itself, making people jump aside. There seemed to be a lot of people out, even though it was cold. Somebody started to yell at the police for parking on the square, but stopped when the policemen got out of their cars in what looked like a coordinated move, their backs straight, their faces set, looking hard and efficient. As Fahima watched, the eight policemen converged on Four Eyes, their weapons drawn.

Fahima rushed inside, her eyes wide. "Oh, Tim! Tim! Come and see!"

The two of them, and nearly everybody else in the depot, went to the big windows overlooking the square to watch, as the police bent Four Eyes over the hood of one of the police cars and searched him, then cuffed his hands behind his back. One policeman read from a little card in his hand, and Tim guessed he was reading Four Eyes his rights.

"I wonder what they think he's done?" he asked no one.

"Plotting the overthrow of the universe," said somebody. There was some nervous laughter, but not much. It was obviously something very serious. Look at the cops. They were tight and tough, totally jacked up.

Then Four Eyes was stuffed into the back of a police car and all the police went away, leaving people wandering around looking at each other questioningly.

"Haven't the cops anything better to do than harass some harmless nut?" The speaker was a middle-aged woman who made the depot her hangout while her husband was in the city being a lawyer. A lot of people agreed with her, but not Tim. He knew better. That had been no roust. Those cops looked too—what? Efficient?

But within minutes, it seemed, the word was out around the square and in the depot itself: Patty had been murdered, some kids had found her head (her *head*!) down in the marsh, along with things belonging to Four Eyes.

When Tim heard the news he began to see black specks in front of his eyes, and he had to go out and sit down against the side of the building. It was horrible. Horrible. And what was worst, Tim had known somehow, had forboded, dreaded this would happen. He had made himself watch out for her, and it had done no good. Patty was dead. Barry was dead. Suddenly and with great horror he thought that both women had been killed by the same man. A serial killer, somebody out there who was killing young women, my God, Barry's head, that one open eye, he could see now in his mind Patty's head, some bastard was hanging around *here*, selecting his victims!

Old Dorothy came out and stood next to Tim. She had her hands under her red apron, folded against her stomach. She did not look down at Tim, but said, "He didn't kill anybody. He ain't a killer."

Tim wanted to agree with her, but the words would not come out. He was confused. He felt terribly guilty. Somehow this killer had taken two women from under Tim's protection and viciously murdered them. It made Tim dizzy and made his heart pound. Why am I having this reaction? he asked himself time and time again, but got no answer. He thought about little Patty, hard-eyed tough little Patty. He could not help himself, he began sobbing, his big hands clutching his knees. He did not care who saw him.

After he did not know how long, he felt that there was someone beside him, and blindly he turned toward her. He knew who it was, who it had to be. He felt her arms around him and her breasts against his cheek.

"Poor P-Patty!" he sobbed like a child.

"Yes, yes," said Fahima gently.

THE police attack on the town square would have been appropriate for the kind of man they thought they were picking up—a man who had savagely murdered two women and might have murdered more. He could have been armed with a gun or knife or other weapon. He might have been crazy as hell, and the police knew from wide experience that one crazy person could hold off five or six big cops. The large number of officers dispatched to the scene was to prevent violence, and was successful in this.

The two policemen who had Four Eyes in the back of their car knew him by sight, and hadn't thought much about him except as another wandering nut who happened to land in their territory, and would probably soon move on. They had been very excited at the capture, but now, with Four Eyes safely handcuffed in the back as they rode north on the freeway toward the county courthouse, they calmed down. He did not seem very dangerous back there.

The driver, who wore glasses himself, said over his shoulder, "What's your real name, son?"

Four Eyes did not answer. He was looking out the window at the profile of the mountain to the west. He was thinking about Patty, about the time they had gone walking on the mountain together, and what a wonderful time they had enjoyed. He forgot that Patty had been sullen and complaining; he forgot that she had gone with him to avoid somebody else. He only remembered the pleasure he had felt at her company, and a terrible regret that she was dead. He knew he had been arrested for murder, but he did not care. It did not matter; nothing mattered. He did not answer the policemen when they talked to him because he did not really hear them.

In the county sheriff's office where he was to be booked, photo-graphed, and fingerprinted, there was a minor ruckus when the two officers brought him in. A drunk was being booked ahead of him, a thickset balding man who was obviously very drunk. He took one look at Four Eyes and yelled, "Oh, hell! Yer not gonna make me sit in jail with this crazy man, are you? God damn! Might as well put me in with a nigger!" This got a laugh from a couple of the deputies. As it happened, the only other man in the drunk tank that day was a gigantic black man. As they processed Four Eyes they heard the white man yell "Son of a bitch!" as he was led into the tank.

Four Eyes was taken upstairs, stripped, and given an orange jump-suit and a pair of cheap tennis shoes that had no laces. He was hand-ed a blanket and a pillow without a pillowcase and led to a small single cell down the row from the felony tank. His cell did not open onto the felony tank. It was feared that the other inmates of the tank might gang up on Four Eyes, injure or even kill him. Prisoners were notoriously violent toward sex offenders.

Four Eyes put the blanket and pillow on the narrow metal rack of the bunk and began to pace the cell, three paces in either direction. He did not think; he only felt his sorrow for Patty. He was, of course, in shock.

Two hours later a deputy came for him and led him down to an office, where he sat opposite a man in a white shirt and striped neck-tie. There was another man in an open shirt and black pants stand-ing there, and the uniformed deputy left. Four Eyes stood silent, not focusing on either man.

"Your name is Wardell James Pittman?" the man at the desk asked him. Four Eyes did not answer. There were some of his things on the desk, and a tape recorder, which was on. Four Eyes could see his plans, rolled up, dirty-looking on the green blotter of the desk.

They told him his rights again, and explained that he did not have to speak if he did not want to. He did not speak. With a sigh, the officer at the desk shut off the tape recorder and pushed a button on his desk. The deputy came in and took Four Eyes back to his cell. Later they came for him again and took him to a blank-looking room with a table and two chairs. There was a man already in the room, a rumpled man with a pipe in his mouth.

"Please sit down, Wardell," the man said. Four Eyes did not sit down. After a while, the man sat. He had a briefcase in front of him. He opened it and then closed it. He told Four Eyes his name and said that he was a lawyer, and could act for Four Eyes, if he wanted. Four Eyes did not speak to the man.

"All right," the man said after a while. He got up and offered to shake hands. Four Eyes did not even look at his hand, but stood there, his eyes unfocused.

"I understand," the man said. "You're pretty shook up. I'll come back later." Four Eyes never saw him again.

They took him back to his cell and brought him his dinner. He did not eat it. The cell had no window, but he stood as if looking out a window, his hands at his sides.

At first the police were jubilant; they thought they had luckily captured a serial killer, even if the MOs were not quite the same, in fact, were not the same at all, except for a couple of telling details: both victims had been around the depot area, and both had been beheaded. They had officers out combing the area looking for the second body, and confidently expected to find it hacked to pieces and spread around. But they never did find the body, and after only a few days most of the working police were beginning to doubt Four Eyes' guilt. They had no evidence for or against, but he just didn't seem the type.

"He's crazy as a hoot owl," was the common opinion. Even if he had committed the murders, he could not be held responsible, they all thought. But that was not how the district attorney's office saw it, and that was not how the sheriff saw it. Even after two psychiatrists had spent time with Four Eyes and reported that he was near catatonic and, in their opinion, crazy as a hoot owl, the district attorney and the sheriff agreed that the case should go forward. Too many of these bastards had gotten off scott free with their God damned psycho defenses, and then gone out blithely to kill more women. They did not want that to happen this time. They tried a couple more doctors, and this pair agreed that Four Eyes, though eccentric, was capable of telling right from wrong and was probably subject to wild rages.

Four Eyes had not actually spoken to them. They had drawn their conclusions mostly from the stuff that was coming in on him; various records from around the country. Wardell James Pittman, they discovered, had enlisted in the army over fifteen years before, and in basic training had been involved in some kind of hazing incident; one the Army preferred not to talk about. The end result had been a medical discharge for Four Eyes, and fifty percent disability payments—cheap at the price. Then Four Eyes had been in and out of mental institutions around the country, with conflicting medical reports. He was crazy, he was not crazy, that was the sum. His plan for sending all the weapons to Venus was pure paranoia, as far as the doctors were concerned.

TIM asked for and got some time off work. He stayed home in bed. He felt as if he had some kind of flu. His wife brought him hot spiced tea with honey in it, as he lay propped against three pillows grimly watching events on the television and reading accounts in the newspapers. It was all bullshit, of course. The only photograph of Four Eyes was a mug shot without his glasses, and he looked properly horrible. And that name: Wardell James Pittman. They always called them by their full names, and this made them seem more guilty, somehow, as if all murders and sex crimes were committed by people who went by their full names.

There were no pictures of Patty except a drawing, and Tim shuddered to think how the artist had made the sketch. In the drawing she did not look hard at all, just young, innocent, and pretty. The sketch appeared in all the papers and on all the news programs and never failed to upset Tim. He could have stopped looking, but he did not. There was something punitive the way he forced himself to follow the story in the press. He wondered for the thousandth time why he felt guilty about things he had not done. He wondered why he had broken down and cried over Patty when the truth was that he hadn't much liked her and had wished she would go away. He was even bothered by the way Fahima had comforted him, although still in his memory the feel of her against him was warm and rich. Of course with Claire waiting on him hand and foot and being so concerned and sympathetic, he felt doubly guilty. Even so he played the scene in his mind over and over, sometimes pretending the pillow hot against his cheek was Fahima's motherly breast. Just like a God damned kid with his first teacher's crush.

When the county homicide detective had questioned them later in the day Tim had been all right, and his authority as manager took over and got him through. He knew nothing to help the police make a case against Four Eyes. He was frank in his belief that Four Eyes couldn't have committed the murder, but the plainclothes cop just looked at him flatly and went on with his questions. Did all policemen now have mustaches? Perhaps so.

Now, lying in bed for the third straight day, Tim began to wonder what was happening to him. Was he slowing down on the job? Was he perhaps burning out as manager? Having owned his own place had spoiled him, perhaps. Or maybe he had allowed himself to sink into the local community too much, so that he cared too much when things like this happened. The case was out of the papers and off the television now, superseded by other horrors in other places. There was no reason for him to stay home in bed. Unless he was trying to avoid Fahima. He loved her, that was a fact. But on their little improvised picnic he hadn't had the guts to make a pass at her, and that is what you did when you were in love. Tim supposed. He had to admit he had never really been in love before. Wasn't that an old song? Or wasn't it all from an old song, and not a very good old song. He could not remember which one, but there had to be an old song about a jerk too timid to assert his love.

Then with a suddenness that amazed his wife Tim was out of bed and in the shower, his fresh work clothes laid out on the bed, checked shirt, tan cords, fresh Jockey shorts, white cotton sweat socks. It was a quick shower, and he was shaved, cologned, and out of there in about ten minutes.

"You must be feeling better," Claire said.

"Can't fart around all week," he said with false cheer. Lying there it had suddenly come to him that if Four Eyes couldn't have done the killings, and the authorities were convinced that he had, then there was a killer out there, drawing on the depot for his potential victims. The police would not be on the alert. All Tim's girls were in danger. Fahima, needless to say, was in danger. Soft, clumsy, inept as he was, Tim had to be there.

But the joke was on him. Today Fahima was off, and as much as he wanted to talk to her, just talk to her, he did not call her at home. Instead he finished the day out working as hard as he could, tackling all the little shit jobs he had been putting off.

The fuss about the killing had not quite died down, and there were lots of people stopping by to have coffee and pick up whatever gossip they could; tourists driving slowly by, clogging the area but not enough to need a policeman. It was really amazing how everything seemed to want to get back to normal, after such a horrible event. Even Tim, by the end of the day, felt that Patty's murder was receding into the past, where it belonged.

For all except poor Four Eyes. Nobody around there really thought he had anything to do with it. "They got the wrong man, as usual," was the rough consensus of the regulars, who now felt that Four Eyes had been one of them. Tim had to laugh.

As it turned out, the only other person from around the square who was picked up, taken north, and questioned, was Nifty Nick. When the local police had been debriefed on possible suspects aside from Four Eyes, Nick's name came up several times. "The story is that he killed a bunch of people in Vietnam and it unhinged the poor fucker," said one cop.

"Yeah," said another. "And he was supposed to have done his killings with a knife."

So they had to at least talk to him. Two cops caught Nick just as he was settling into his evening's drinking with the boys. It was a chilly evening, and Nick wore his old stained worn foul-weather jacket, his hands stuffed down into the pockets. The two cops came up to where the boys were sitting, bottles now concealed. They politely asked Nick if he would step over to the vehicle with them and answer a few questions, "about this mess with the girl."

Nick nodded silently, his little mouth tight under his mustache and tangled beard, his eyes frightened as usual. At the police car they asked Nick where he had been the night the girl disappeared, and Nick shrugged and started to move away, but one of the police said, "Look, they want to talk to you up at the county courthouse, just take a little of your time," and Nick was more or less forced into the car. No cuffs were used, but one of the officers got into the back with him, while the other drove.

Nick said nothing on the way up, and said nothing to the detectives who interrogated him. He just sat in his chair across the desk and looked scared. He did not even tell them his name.

"Doesn't anybody from around there know how to talk?" asked one detective humorously.

"We could throw the little fucker in the tank for a couple days," somebody suggested, but the detective frowned.

"No reason. Just take him on back."

So Nick was waiting in the corridor for the police to run him back down to the square when they brought Four Eyes by, escorted by a deputy. The deputy and Four Eyes stopped at the elevator, right next to Nifty Nick. Nick and Four Eyes looked at each other.

"Hello," said Four Eyes to Nick. It was the first thing he had said, as far as anybody knew.

Nick's eyes bulged as if it took tremendous effort for him to speak. Then, just as the elevator doors opened, he said to Four Eyes, "You didn't kill nobody."

"Come on, Four Eyes," the deputy said. Nobody called him by his name anymore.

T HE deputy reported that Four Eyes had finally spoken, but until Mark Dakin, the young lawyer, appeared on the scene Four Eyes continued to remain silent, except for that one "Hello." Dakin did not work for the public defender's office. All the public defenders had heavy work loads, and, frankly, none of them wanted the case, and used Four Eyes' silence as a way of getting out of it. Dakin was only a couple of years out of law school, a smiling, curly-haired young man. His dinky office was only a couple of blocks from the depot, over a second-hand furniture mart (whose back-room toilet he used).

Nobody was beating his door down, he knew the depot scene, and in fact was a regular drinker of *caffe latte,* which he carried up to his office in a big white plastic cup to drink while he read the morning paper. So when the judge called him and asked if he would see Four Eyes he not only agreed, he drove up to the county building with a rising sense of expectation.

When Four Eyes was brought in to the attorney's visiting room, Mark Dakin was seated at the bare oak table with his briefcase at his feet and his hands neatly folded in front of him.

"Please sit down," he said to Four Eyes, who sat down. "I've been asked to speak to you about representing you in court. I know you haven't spoken to anybody around here, but I hope you'll speak to me."

Four Eyes said nothing, but Dakin thought there was a hint of amusement in his eyes. Dakin knew that nobody around the depot thought he was guilty. He had not made up his own mind yet. What he had read about serial killers did not clear things up much; apparently, they could be from any walk of life, be any kind of person. Seeing Four Eyes close up didn't help. He could be a killer, could be innocent as a lamb. It did not matter to the State, Dakin knew. The State wanted Four Eyes found guilty and put in prison, right now. They wanted no fucking nonsense about insanity, either. As far as Dakin could see, the defense attorney's job was simply to keep the State from having too easy a time railroading Four Eyes.

He explained this to Four Eyes carefully. "Whether you talk or not, they can try you and probably convict you. I haven't seen their evidence yet, but I know the basic setup, and a lot of people have done a lot of time on less. Look, you don't have to speak to them, but you will have to speak with your attorney. Do you understand? Hey, just nod your head or something."

But Four Eyes just sat, with his hands in his lap. Dakin did think he saw some slight question in his eyes. You really couldn't tell much, with those milkbottle-bottoms he used for glasses, smeary with fingerprints and God knows what else.

"Hey," Dakin said gently, "I need this case. I need you to say you want me for your lawyer. You don't have to say anything else to them, and to me you can say anything at all. I want to help you, and as I said, I need the work." He grinned and scratched his chin—it had started as a con, but the truth was, he did need the case. Not for the money, which wasn't much, but because he was going nuts sitting around.

"Every time my brother calls I tell him I'm too busy to talk," he said, wondering why he had said it. "But he sees right through me. Always has, always will, I guess."

"All right," Four Eyes said. His voice was rusty, and he coughed a couple of times.

"Do you want me for your lawyer?"

"All right."

"Will you tell them?"

"All right."

"Okay, that's great. Ha, this is pretty exciting. Now, before we make our big announcement, let's you and me talk a little. First, how come you don't want to talk?"

He had worried about this, because it was a dumb but obvious way to try for an insanity defense—especially easy since you said nothing incriminating, by saying nothing at all. Dakin hoped Four Eyes wasn't that stupid.

Four Eyes sat a moment, as if composing himself, and then with a smile he said, "I know this sounds funny, but I don't think they have any right to do this to me. I did nothing. They have no right to hold me. Oh, I know they are going to do it, and I know they think they're doing the right thing. But I can't cooperate with them. So I decided not to talk to them."

"Cooperating with me would not be the same as cooperating with them," Dakin said quickly. "I'm on your side. You can tell me everything that happened, and it will go no farther. That's the law."

"I know I have to have a lawyer," Four Eyes said.

"If you killed her, I have to know now. And I have to know everything about it. If you didn't, I have to know where you were, what you were doing, everything, around the time of death."

He stopped talking because tears were running down Four Eyes' cheeks. Dakin waited patiently. He knew now that Four Eyes was innocent. He did not know how he knew, hell, tears were easy enough, any country psychopath could cry you a river on command. No, it was something else. Whatever it was, Mark Dakin was convinced. He waited a while and then handed Four Eyes a Kleenex from his pocket.

Four Eyes wiped his face and said, "I won't do that again."

"It's okay," said Dakin. "You liked her pretty much, huh?"

"She was starting to like me, too. I know that. But I won't talk to them."

"You don't have to. The right to remain silent."

"I want to go now."

They shook hands and Four Eyes was taken away. Dakin felt good. He talked to the people in the prosecuting attorney's office and told Darwin, the guy handling the case, that Four Eyes would probably never speak to them, certainly wouldn't testify, and was probably innocent as a baby.

"Fat fucking chance," said Darwin.

"Well, there'll be no fucking chance you boys are going to railroad him," he said rather too cockily. But he was feeling good. This was just the kind of case he wanted. He and he alone could save Four Eyes.

But as he drove back down the freeway he wondered if there wasn't something he didn't know yet, something important. Something Four Eyes was saving up.

FAHIMA's lunch break started out badly—at least for Tim. There was an Iranian, maybe thirty-five or forty, little short guy around five-six, shiny hair, muddy eyes, and a sensual leer pasted on his mouth. He liked to come in and stand at the counter, looking over the pastries and croissants at Fahima as she worked, talking to her in Farsi.

"Is he a fellow Iranian?" Tim asked politely one day. "A student?"

"He is real estate man," Fahima said.

"He likes you," Tim said.

The trouble was, Fahima seemed to like him, too. She smiled and talked back to the guy in her native language, and it was clear from her expression that she was not above a little harmless flirtation. The guy must have known he was too old, too short, and too ugly for her. And that she was married to Hassan, who if he ever came around and saw the guy flirting with his wife would probably take him apart.

One day this guy was hanging around when it was time for Fahima to take her lunch break. Tim was sitting at his little table trying to work out a new schedule for Thursdays, since one of the kids had quit abruptly. He saw Fahima with her paper plate of food head out the back door onto the square. The morning had been foggy, but now it was nice out there. The trouble was, the Iranian real estate asshole followed her.

Tim threw down his ballpoint pen in disgust, and looked around at nobody. He was pretty angry, even though he had no right to be. He found himself looking angrily at Four Eyes' lawyer, Mark Dakin, who had been hanging around sucking up *lattes* and trying to get information to help his case. The lawyer grinned weakly at Tim and said, "If looks could kill, hey, Boss?"

Talking like that, Tim wondered how good a lawyer he could be. Tim grinned at the man falsely and said, "Gloomy thoughts," and got up and went out the back door, suddenly sneezing in the sunlight.

There she was, sitting in a halo of light, modestly eating her lunch. And right next to her, pleading his case, was the Iranian. Tim found himself walking over to join them. But just before he got there, the Iranian guy jumped up and went away, without looking at Tim. Fahima smiled up at Tim and patted the concrete beside her.

Tim sat, but instead of the meaningless pleasantry he meant to make, said, "Who is that guy, anyway? What does he want?"

Fahima laughed and looked at him over her turkey sandwich as she bit into it. Tim waited impatiently while she chewed. Finally, she said, "He wants to take me out. For dinner."

Dinner and a fuck, Tim thought, but wisely did not say. "Does he know you're married?"

"Oh, yes. He knows Hassan. It does not matter to him."

Tim sat and watched her eat. She seemed unconcerned about this man, or about anything. He should calm down. But it was hard for him to calm down. He was worried about her no matter what she did. Most of the people around there had stopped thinking about the killer, assuming finally that Four Eyes must have done it, or nobody did it, it just happened, they went on about their lives. Like sheep. Or wild antelope. He remembered seeing on television some footage shot on the veldt in Africa, a bunch of herd animals like antelope, kudu, gnus, what have you, quietly feeding while a lion walked among them. Stupid fucking animals.

"Fahima," he said abruptly. "I can't believe you're going home in less than a month."

There was nothing to say to this, so she did not speak. But Tim went on, going over very old material. Fahima did not understand how things must have changed over there. The religious nuts were in charge. They would see right through her. She would be in extreme danger of jail or worse. Etc.

At last she turned her large serious eyes on him and said, "Oh, Tim, you could not understand."

"I understand, all right," he said angrily. Why was he suddenly angry? "You're gonna throw your life away for a bunch of people who don't know you and don't give a damn about you. And even if you win your revolution, what then? Do you know what they do with the revolutionaries after the revolution? They round 'em up and kill 'em, that's what. Nobody wants them around. Shit-disturbers."

"Shit disturbers," she said. "What does that mean?"

"Too hard to explain," he said. "Look, one last time, won't you consider staying here? You know your family can arrange it."

"But why? Why stay? What is there for me here?"

"There's me," Tim said, and the cat was forever out of the bag. And as long as the bag was open:

"I love you. God damn it."

"Oh, Tim, please," she said. She did not seem shocked or angry, only concerned.

"I know it's hopeless," he said hopelessly. "But I love you."

Roberta, one of the kitchen workers, came out on the square, her red apron like a flag. Tim was wanted on the phone by the electrician. Tim said he would call the man back. Roberta smiled, said the weather seemed to be getting a little better and she hoped it wouldn't be one of those typically foggy summers. Tim agreed, wanting to yell at her to get back to work, but kept it in, and soon Roberta went inside.

After a thick silence, Fahima said in a low voice, "You don't really mean that. Americans say that all the time to people."

"Yeah, it's like a form of hello," he said with real bitterness. He should never have spoken up. She was sorry for him, but that was all. He felt pretty bad.

"I don't even know what the hell I'm talking about," he said with some confusion. "You're in as much danger here as you would be there, I guess. Maybe not."

"What do you mean?"

"Oh, nothing. I hope I haven't wrecked your day."

She took his hand. Hers was soft and warm, comforting. His was, thank God, warm and dry. Their hands fitted together in a way that made Tim want to cry. But he did not. She was about to speak:

"I am not free," she said.

What the hell, thought Tim. "Hassie? He'd probably be glad not to have to go back. If you left him. Oh, what the hell am I talking about?"

"Yes, what the hell," she said, but with sympathy. "But you have Hassan wrong. He is important man at home. He will be officer, and will work among junior officers. Very much more important than me."

"But you talked him into this, didn't you?"

She smiled almost sadly. "No," she said. "You do not understand Hassan. When we met, he was most brilliant student of Marxism. Most brilliant theoretician. Did I say that right?"

"Yeah," Tim said, having shot his Irish wad. How could he now get his pride back? Was there no way? Oh, the hell with it. He stood.

She stood beside him. Their hands were still clasped. She was very close to him. She looked up, serious, and said, "I like you very much, Tim. You are my favorite American. If things were different. . ." Neither of them knew how long they stood looking into each other. But when they heard somebody say, "Romance at the depot, how quaint," they laughed, and Tim got his hand back and gave her a pop on the shoulder, comradely pop.

"Gotta get back to work," he said.

"Oh, Tim, what can I say?"

Oh, yes, really. What *do* you say, when the player comes dragging back to the dugout having most resoundingly struck out? Better luck next time? *Shit!*

MARK Dakin liked hanging around the depot. It was better than sitting in his office reading case law and waiting for the telephone to ring. This way his answering machine could do all the waiting, and he could sit here drinking the expensive but delicious *caffe lattes* and watching the local pussy parade by. It was especially nice when the morning fog had dissipated and the girls would come out in their scanty summer garments. Dakin was an ass-man, unashamed, and liked to sit at the table just across from where people lined up at the counter. This way he was eye-level with a lot of fine asses. Especially now in summer the young girls would come in wearing shorts that had apparently been fitted on them by the editors of *Playboy* magazine. *Playboy* was Dakin's favorite magazine. *Quality.*

Otherwise not much was doing. Four Eyes had been indicted for the murder of Jane Doe *aka* Patty. The severed head and the missing body went against him for a lesser charge than murder. Not logically. Actually. Mark Dakin had long since stopped expecting logic out of the law. The Barry Latimer charges had been dropped, since there wasn't a shred of evidence to connect Four Eyes to the crime.

But the State was real serious about the other charge. Dakin's discovery motion had discovered nothing that hadn't been in the papers, meaning the State didn't have a whole hell of a lot to go on, and was counting on jury rage to do its work. What did they really have? The head at his campsite, evidence of flight, although the poor bastard only fled to the depot. Witnesses who had seen them together around here and hiking on the mountain. And his silence. Four Eyes could not plead insanity because he wasn't guilty. He could only plead not guilty, and he did, through Mark Dakin. Dakin had no witnesses. What would they testify to? "Seemed like a harmless nut to me . . ."

Neither of the dead women had anybody behind them to press for a better investigation. Barry Latimer's family hired a local lawyer to take care of the body, and that had been all. Patty remained un-identified, and a really weird thing happened when nobody claimed her head. Something Dakin would not have known about if he hadn't started hanging out in the depot.

The old woman, Dorothy, had apparently heard that no one claimed Patty's remains, so she said something like, "Aw, hell, I'll take it." Called up, bickered about price, got the head cremated and picked it up in a little bronze urn that the old woman complained cost too damned much for just the small amount of ashes in it. Then, apparently, as the story went, she got a friend with an open car to drive her up on the mountain, where, probably after looking around furtively, she dumped the ashes out into the breeze. The urn she threw into an ashcan. "What the hell use is it?"

Dakin liked the old woman for that, even though she would not give him the time of day, frowned at him like she frowned at every-body. She would have made a lousy character witness.

As it was, Dakin was going to have to rely on his powers of cross-examination, and his spellbinding ability at summing-up time. Ha ha. Poor Four Eyes. Dakin knew what he was up against. People wanted all these killings stopped, and they hardly cared if some harmless bum got nailed in the process. Nor did they seem to mind that the real killer was still apparently on the loose. Unless he was locked up somewhere else for something else, as so often happened in these cases.

Dakin enjoyed talking to Tim as he sat at his own little table not far away and worked on his papers. Tim was a nice guy, very open, very friendly, and who obviously had faith in Four Eyes' innocence.

Then one day Dakin said lazily to Tim, "I guess the best thing that could happen for poor old Four Eyes is for the real killer to behead another of the girls around here." Tim's face wrinkled up with such obvious outrage that for a thrilling second Dakin thought, *"He's the one, by God!"*

But no. After hanging out for a while, he could see that old Tim was nuts about Fahima, the big tall Iranian girl, whose ass was small and neat, even though her shoulders would lead you to believe that she would have a big broad ass. Great figure. Nice-looking woman overall, but Dakin made no passes. He was content to look. And have his fantasies. Dakin had incredible fantasies, if he said so himself.

Dakin's visits to Four Eyes were somehow touching. The man seemed to have gotten over the worst of his pain at the death of Patty, and often spent most of their time together working on his plan, which he carried around with him everywhere. The authorities had not given back his original set of plans, so Four Eyes had started a new set, funny little drawings of rocket ships, bombs, people, words you could hardly make out, stars, planets, moons. And talk? The man talked a blue streak. He would talk to anybody except the opposition; he had disciplined himself to evade their tricks with a nod and a grin, but no outbursts of speech. Dakin had to admire him for that. They planted cellmates on him and everything, but all Four Eyes would talk about was his plan, which nobody wanted to hear about, or his new cause of prison reform, which nobody wanted to hear about.

"This place is terrible," Four Eyes said cheerfully to Mark Dakin one day. It was right after his trial date had been set, and Dakin had volunteered to make some delays.

"What for?" said Four Eyes. "I know I'll be convicted. I know that's what they want. Pretty soon I'll be going into the prison system and it's much worse than this place. I've been held in some pretty bad places, but this prison system is the worst. Nobody should be in it. Nobody."

Dakin could not resist: "What about the guy who really killed Patty?"

Four Eyes looked pretty upset for a moment, but then came out of it. "That guy," he said. "He's made me hate him. I even want to kill him. Myself, with my hands. Sometimes I dream about it, killing him. And that's what I'm *against*. But even he doesn't deserve prison. I hate him, he's done that to me, but it's against everything I believe. See the mess he's causing?"

That was the end of that meeting. Four Eyes seemed confused and angry now, and Dakin got out of there and into the clean fresh air.

THE time was drawing close. Another week of work, then a week of packing and madness, then Fahima and Hassan would be gone. No more America. After six years of happiness, it would be a wrenching pain to leave. And most painful to leave Tim.

At first he had been like a father—not like *her* father, who had spent most of his life in an opium haze, which the Shia fanatics had outlawed so that her father had had to enter a hospital and dry out—Fahima had not seen him since he had been off the drug, and had been told that he spent most of his time with his older friends, talking about religion. No, not that kind of father, not a real father but an ideal one. She had found herself looking forward to coming to work when she knew Tim would be there, and then she knew that she cared for him more than she should.

She had hurt him the time she had called him her favorite American. She had been trying to say that to her he was like an American god, with all the charming and wonderful American weaknesses and none of the terrible weaknesses, greed and coldheartedness, selfishness and ignorance. Of course these were not exclusively American traits, but they were part of the America, the world, that she had chosen to spend the rest of her life fighting.

And to say good-bye to Tim without mentioning her love for him. Because what do you say? Yes, I love you, too, more than I want to, and good-bye forever. It was too sad. Better to part friends.

But on this lovely sunny day, she wanted to say a private good-bye. She asked for a few extra minutes on her lunch break, "to do a few little things," and walked by herself up the street to the park.

Soon she was under the redwoods, marvelling again at the remarkable light shining down from the branches, turning the creek from brown to shining silver, transforming everything with its silence, creating within people a sense of religious awe. She was awed, yes, but not religiously. There was no God, only nature, but that was enough.

Slowly she walked through the playground section, where mothers sat in sunshine patches watching their children enjoy the swings and slides. She was tempted to sit on one of the swings. It had been a long time since she had been for a good swing—she and Hassan in Boston, in a snowy deserted playground, Hassan pushing her exuberantly until she almost fell out of the swing. And then they had gone home to their tiny apartment off Scollay Square and made love for hours and hours. Hassan was not only brilliant and brave, he was a magnificent lover.

She walked on, thinking fondly of Hassan. But it was not for him, her husband, that she finally rejected the notion of staying in America. She was committed. If she did not go home now she would be a traitor, not only to her cause but to herself, and that she would never be. But oh, it was a temptation! To stay with Tim, have babies, enjoy pleasures, and forget the world! Ah! But of course no. Finally no. She knew she was not noble. She did what she did because all the forces in her life directed her to. In the press of her work and her life, she would gradually idealize and then ultimately forget Tim. That was the way, she knew.

Here was their little picnic grove, where they had been happy one afternoon. It was a beautiful place, filled with peace, the soft redwood smell, that incredible light, making the picnic table glow with significance. She was going to sit on the picnic table and think warmly about Tim, but something caught just the corner of her eye, a movement in among the trees, and everything in her came screaming alert as she saw quickly moving through light and shadows the green clothes of the man who frightened her, adrenaline rushing through her body as he broke into the open, his eyes mad, his mouth in a fixed horrible crooked grin, a fluttering flash of light in his hand.

Fahima's mind worked as rapidly as it ever had. It told her that the man was very much stronger than she, was carrying a knife, that he meant to kill her. She did not actually see the knife, only the flashing, but that was enough. This was not the battleground: she must run. Fahima turned and fled, running through the park as fast as she could, as fast as any gazelle, her mind no longer working, in a panic of terror. She had never felt anything like it. It filled her; she could not do anything but give in to the terror, to run blindly. The rationality of her act vanished under the animal panic, and she escaped.

Tim was trying to get the toaster to work by taking it apart and putting it back together. If this did not work, he did not know what he would do with the goddamned thing. The place was busy around him, and naturally there were several people demanding toast, so Tim was not in the best of moods. Fahima had gone somewhere, he did not know where, and that made him uneasy. As he worked and fended off questions and bantered with customers, his mind was elsewhere, with Fahima, who had crossed the street, he knew, going in the direction of the park. The park. Maybe, maybe, aw, who was he to think that? Why would she? He grinned to himself; it was the kind of thing he would do, make a pilgrimage to the picnic place . . . But then something else flashed across his mind, something half-seen, half-felt, and his hands dropped the toaster, breaking it forever.

He was out of there, empty mind, panic-filled heart, running wildly up the street, bowling people over, acting like a madman, bursting into the park and running silently over the springy carpet of redwood needles, thinking against thought that he was too late, he was always too late, bursting into their grove to see nothing, no one. Empty.

Tim stood panting like an animal. Nobody. Nothing. He could feel his face redden. What stupidity! He panted heavily. He shouldn't do such things, he was too old. He could have pulled a muscle easily, fallen on his face, broken a hipbone, anything. He thought about sitting down and resting, but no, he would walk back and let the slow walk put his breath back in him. He made his way to the street, not far away, and saw the guy in green, leaning against his van, that God damned van, panting. He looked as tired as Tim.

"What the fuck are you doing?" Tim demanded.

"What the fuck do you care?" came the answer. The guy grinned that nasty grin and Tim wanted to powder him. But what for? Tim must have seen the van going past the depot and registered it unconsciously. That had been what must have triggered him into action. It was pretty embarrassing, especially with this prick grinning at him. Without another word, Tim headed back for the depot.

But something in him told him to stop at the storeroom. Fahima would be there, he was certain. And she was, sitting on some cartons, her hands on her knees. She looked terrible. Her face white, her eyes unnaturally large.

"What's the matter?" Tim asked her.

"Nothing," she said. "I felt a little sick. I will be fine."

"What happend out there?" he demanded.

"Nothing," she said finally. "Nothing."

She had to say that. She could not tell him what she had imagined. She could not tell him of the terror. She had defended terrorism too many times. Tim had argued with her too many times, and she had implied he was naive too many times. Now, with the terror still receding, that mad implacable face still grinning in her mind, she wanted only peace. Time later to think about what she had learned about herself. Now, with Tim staring down at her accusingly, she could not believe that the man had actually come after her. He had stepped out of the trees and she had panicked.

"I am late," she said, and got to her feet. She and Tim were very close, and if he had kissed her, she would have been glad. But he turned abruptly instead and flung open the storeroom door.

"Ladies first," he said bitterly.

THE whole episode rattled Dick pretty badly for a few days. He went where he was dispatched, did his work, but otherwise tried to keep pretty much out of sight. He could remember the whole thing pretty well, and it scared him to think how close he had come to total disaster. Going after that broad right out in the open. Nuts. Totally nuts. He could remember being so excited he damned near busted open with it. She was a tasty one, that bitch, and he had been watching her, watching her, making plans, having dreams . . . This was going to be so much better than Barry or Patty, where he had been so fucked up he had gone out of control and almost spoiled the fun. He had blanked on Barry, couldn't admit to himself that he had actually gone and done it, then blanked on Patty for a few days, had dreams about her. But deep down he knew he had done it, and done it badly. This time, with the big one, he could remember everything except a couple of seconds there when he must have had a purple flash or something—anyway when he came out of it she was gone and Wimp City, her boss, was standing there looking at him cross-eyed. Tim didn't bother Dick, not personally anyway, but Dick went home and spent that evening after supper agonizing over his knife collection, and finally decided to get rid of it. He packed them all on their cardboard hanger-racks in the back of the van and took them out to this place he knew over the edge of the big bay and dumped them in. Just as he had done with Patty's body, only with the body he had been sure there was an outgoing tide, and bye bye Baby.

But time passed and nobody came around. The cops hadn't talked to him since the routine questioning on Patty, and even then they had only been trying to build a case against Four Eyes. Dick hadn't cooperated. He didn't know a fucking thing. Why get involved? Anyway, time passed and Dick found himself drawn back to the square, to look over the crop. He was no longer interested in the big girl from the depot, Fatima or whatever the hell her name was.

No, you couldn't even say he was looking, really. Just hanging out. He wasn't quite easy enough to enter the depot and order an egg salad sandwich, but he stood on the edge of the square that afternoon, hands in his pockets, watching the passing parade, especially some of the cute high school girls who were wasting their afternoons downtown instead of at the beach. He thought about the beach, but there was too much traffic on these nice summer days. Fuck it. This was just fine.

Until that little nut Milos started getting on his case. He didn't even notice him at first, then he saw that Milos was circling him at long range, and talking, pretty loud.

"You got somethin' to say?" Dick asked.

"Ha ha, you crazy!" Milos shouted at him. He hit the bricks with his stick and did a little dance. "I saw you!" he almost screamed. "I saw you wit' knife!"

"Buzz off, fuckface," Dick said to him. He felt crawly. What the hell did the guy mean?

"Knife! Knife! I saw knife! You crazy fuck!"

Dick started for the little man, to shut him up. Milos laughed wildly, backing away, not running, just keeping Dick at bay. "You crazy man! You da guy!"

"Shut your fucking mouth, you little crud!" Dick said angrily. He was really getting mad, this little fuck was mouthing off too much, he had to be shut up. Others watched with obvious amusement while Dick tried unsuccessfully to catch the shouting, gesticulating Milos. Around and around the square they went.

Tim, counting pieces of carrot cake, as was his duty, happened to look up and see Dick chasing Milos. For some reason, this made him lose his temper. He had been in a state for days anyway, cross and moody at home, busy and not very friendly at work. But now here was that bastard again. Once again Tim wished desperately he had some real reason to call the cops on the guy, but he didn't, and he wasn't going to call them just because he hated the guy. What evidence did he have? None. Oh, he probably wasn't the killer, but Tim sure hated him anyway. Now he was out there chasing poor harmless Milos. Fucking bully. That just about tore it. Tim had taken just about all the shit he could take. He went out the back doors, which stuck sometimes, and stuck now, but he just went through them, and the big glass-panelled doors exploded off their hinges. He was out on the square now, moving toward the guy in green.

Milos shouted to Tim, "He da one! I saw da knife!"

Tim knew instantly that Milos was telling the truth. Angry before, he was now in a passion of rage. It was delicious, after holding himself in for so long. Ah! Now to rip the guy's heart out!

Dick was certainly not afraid of Tim, the fucking wimp, but even wimps could go crazy, and this was a crazy man coming at him. Dick was no coward, but he knew when he was overmatched. He backed away rapidly from the advancing Tim.

"You pissvomit!" Tim yelled insanely. Dick tripped and fell back, and with a yell of pleasure Tim got to him just as he was getting up and smashed him right in the face, knocking him back down. The pain in Tim's hand was nothing. He kicked the down man hard, kicked him again, pulled him to his feet and planted another one right on his nose. The blood fairly sprayed out, and while Dick looked down in horror at his own blood, Tim got him one in the belly. Down he went with an *oof!*

Tim pulled Dick to his feet and got his neck in the crook of his arm, hitting him hard on the right kidney a few times. Dick screamed and tried to say, "Stop!" but the arm choked him and all he did was make a high screaming sound.

"You pigfucker!" Tim yelled. "If I ever catch you around here again. . ." He did not finish, but lifted Dick high over his head and threw him down on the hard bricks. Dick lay beaten, his hands up, his knees drawn up, the picture of a defeated animal. But Tim was not having any of that. He kicked the down man in the ribs and heard a satisfying *crack!*

"Get up and take your medicine," Tim panted.

"I can't!" Dick said. His own blood was all over his face and dripping into his mouth. His eyes were like a cow's eyes at slaughter time.

"Get up or I'll kick your face," Tim said, ready to do just that. Dick got up. "Now get outta here!" Tim demanded, and Dick ran, limped, to his van. Nobody around there ever saw him again.

Tim stood panting, sanity gradually returning. He felt fine. He had done all a civilized man could do. And if he ever saw that fucker again, he *would* kill him.

Tim felt lucky. He had not broken his hand or even jammed a knuckle on that scumbug. His hand hurt a little and there were some scrapes, but no swelling. He had blood all over his clothes and some on his face and in his hair, but none of it was his, and he had to go home anyway to get his toolbox. Lucky again, the doors had come off their hinges but neither of the plate glass panels had broken. One had a small crack near the bottom, but nothing to get excited about.

Claire was concerned but asked no more questions after Tim had said happily that he had been in a little fight. When he got out of the shower he found fresh clothes laid out for him. He dressed quickly and got his toolbox out of the garage and went back down to the depot. There was no fuss. Things were normal, except for the broken doors, lying against the building where Tim had left them. What was needed here was a new set of hinges and hingepins, easily gotten from the hardware store. The doors were made of good wood, that was a blessing, and even though the screws had been ripped out, there was still plenty of solid wood to set the new hinges into.

With some help Tim had the doors rehung by midafternoon. It seemed as if it should be later, but Fahima and the old woman were just getting off. Fahima was due to leave in just days—hours, really, if you wanted to count the hours—and she had a lot of things to do. Tim had not spoken to her alone since the fight, if you could call it a fight, more of a beating, to Tim's way of thinking, since the guy in green hadn't landed a blow or even started one. But he had seen the look on her face. Was it admiration? Speculation? He did not know.

But his lightness of heart passed as he thought: she has only one more shift. Then she is gone.

Fahima was in her turquoise sweatshirt and jeans. She came out of the little closet carrying her shoulder bag. Dorothy and Fahima kissed at the door, then the old woman left.

"I have so much to do," Fahima said to Tim, coming up to him in front of the counter.

"I know," he said inanely. They looked at each other, and something happened. Tim never knew quite what it was, but he found her hands in his, and he was close enough to smell her hair, the clean smell of her hair, and without thinking he said, "The storeroom," and she nodded. He held the door open for her and followed her out onto the street. Sparrows flew up into the tree and a horn honked, there were people on the street, Tim seemed to know them all; everything was in sharp detail, his senses more alive than they had ever been. Walking so close they kept bumping into each other, they began to cross the wide street to the building where the storeroom was. They would make love there, on the floor, on gunnysacks, on boxes, it did not matter. Their moment had come; they had earned it. If Tim could get nothing for his love but this one moment of lovemaking, well, that was that. He was not thinking, only moving toward the storeroom.

Fahima was saturated with love for Tim, and in these moments was not at all sure what would happen in the future. She had lost her strong control over herself and was deliciously helpless in the hands of her emotions, her love for this big American who thought so little of himself and was such a great man.

They were almost across the street when out of nowhere the thought came to Tim's mind, loudly, sharply, almost a spoken voice: *No! I will not betray my wife!*

Tim stopped, stunned.

"What is the matter?" Fahima asked, turning to him. A car made its way around them. Fahima at that moment felt within herself a sudden great harmony with Tim, and the future was once again as planned. She knew what he knew.

"I don't have to take you anyplace to kiss you good-bye," Tim said, and wrapped her in his arms and kissed her. He did not know how long the kiss lasted; there were horns honking, people yelling, even some applause, but that was all somewhere else. Afterward they looked at each other, still holding on tight. "I love you," Tim said to her for the last time.

"Oh, I love you, Tim," she said to him for the first and last time.

And that would be all for them; but it was enough.

Driving home once again that day, Tim thought about his favorite poem in high school, Keats' "Ode on a Grecian Urn." He was not sure he could remember the last of it correctly, but the way he remembered it was the way he felt, and it was a fine, a wonderful, a life-lasting way to feel:

"Bold lover, ever, ever wilt thou love,
And she be fair."

SUMMER was over before Four Eyes had his trial, Fahima and Hassan gone to Persia, never to be seen or heard from by anybody around the depot; new employees coming and going, new people on the square, all under a clear brilliant autumn sky that promised eternal sunshine. The trial only lasted a few days; even jury selection had been accomplished in almost record time. Mark Dakin was not surprised by the speed of things. He had nothing to offer in defense. All he could do was cross-examine the State's witnesses and hope to create some doubt in the minds of the jurors. But this was a chore. The witnesses were all honest people, and the jurors, also honest people, seemed to have turned against Four Eyes right at the beginning, during the parade of police and scientific witnesses.

It wasn't much of a case. Instead of a weapon, the State had witnesses who testified that they had seen Four Eyes with a straight razor, and a criminologist who testified that the severing of Patty's head could have been done with a straight razor. Or the barrel of a Colt .45, thought Dakin sarcastically. They had witnesses who had seen Four Eyes and Patty together, both on the square and on the mountain, even in the depot. They had the boys who had found Patty's head and they had the mute evidence of Four Eyes' camp.

Since Four Eyes would not offer a defense, Dakin had no real choices and by summing-up time he was pretty burned out. There had been no publicity, the papers were full of bigger, more sensational cases, and even the regular courtroom hangers-on favored other courtrooms in the county building. The only regular spectator was Nifty Nick, who hardly missed a day. He would sit right behind

Four Eyes, and although they nodded at each other, they never seemed to speak. Nick would leave the courtroom from time to time, to nip at the pint in his pocket. He looked drunker and drunker as the day went on, but never caused a disturbance, although Dakin could smell his breath and wished he would go away. He did not understand what the goddamn bum was doing there in the first place.

It was easy enough to understand, for Nick anyway. He knew Four Eyes was innocent. In fact, Four Eyes was about the only innocent guy Nick had ever run across, and he came to the trial to watch what they did with an innocent guy. It all went about the way Nick figured it would, with the jury out five hours and returning a verdict of guilty. As Nick knew they would. Nick had committed a lot of murders, and so of course they gave him the Silver Star. He kept it in his pocket to remind him never to trust anybody who had the slightest authority.

Nick hitchhiked to and from the courthouse, and was picked up by the cops a couple of times before the word got out and they stopped bothering him. The cops mostly thought Four Eyes had gotten a bad deal, but it was not the first bad deal they had seen go down, and would not be the last. Everybody around the courthouse seemed to be satisfied with the results of the trial, even Four Eyes, who finally sprang his secret at the time of sentencing.

Tim read it in the one paper that carried an account of the trial, and felt very bad for Four Eyes. The poor guy had waited patiently through all this just so he could get up in front of the world and make his statement, his proposal, his plan for sending all the weapons off the planet. In the paper it said he had made "a garbled plea for world peace," and then the judge sentenced him to life in prison.

Tim had done what he could. He had gone to Dakin and told him about Dick, the guy in green, and how Milos had said he had a knife. Dakin had spoken to Fahima just before she left, but Fahima could not say positively that the guy had a knife, or even that he was after her, only that he had appeared out of the trees (as Tim had suspected, but she had never told him). So all they had were suspicions and Milos. Milos could not be found, and would have made an incredibly bad witness anyway, even if he could have been persuaded to testify. So that all went for nothing, and the case rolled on, and over Four Eyes.

Dakin said good-bye to his client just before they took him to prison. Four Eyes seemed healthy and not at all broken up about the verdict. Of course he had said all along that they were going to convict him. But he didn't even seem upset that his message had not, after all, gone out to the world.

"Well, you have to keep trying," he said. "The main thing now to work for is closing these prisons."

Finally, Dakin had to admire the guy. Old Four Eyes would have been happy to be the last guy let out of prison, if that's what it would take.

"Do you need anything?" asked Dakin hopelessly.

"No," Four Eyes smiled. "My disability money is plenty in here. I'm just fine."

Four Eyes was sent into the prison system and assigned a prison right there in the same county. He was placed in "C" Block, a form of protective solitary confinement. It was felt that the other prisoners might attack or even kill him if he were placed on the line. He exercised one hour a day, alone, walking up and down the small courtyard outside his block. One nice thing, from there he could see the mountain, in different profile, but the same mountain he had so enjoyed walking on and looking at when he had been a free man. He always said hello to the mountain when he came out into the yard, even if it was obscured by fog or clouds, but he was content in the knowledge that the mountain could not hear him.

He was busy. He worked on his two plans—one to get rid of the weapons, the other to close all the prisons—and he talked about these things to the few people he was allowed to talk to. He ate as well as he could, exercised a lot, and bought vitamins at the commissary. He wanted to keep up his health because he knew if he didn't, he might get depressed and lose faith in himself. If he lost faith, he might also lose purpose, and then his life would have no meaning. Four Eyes did not want that to happen.

Milos finally showed up on the square a couple of months after Four Eyes had been convicted. It was early in the morning and still pretty dark when the old woman came out the back doors to smoke her joint and have a bit of peace before the day began. There was Milos, alone in the middle of the square, posing with his stick held high. The old woman watched him quietly for a few moments, and then pinched her joint between her thumb and forefinger, put it into her apron pocket, and went back inside.

A few minutes later, Sherman the town drunk came out of the darkness dressed in his yellow slicker, his face ravaged, and knocked three times on the back door. He sat down on one of the old wooden chairs and waited emptily. In a few moments the old woman brought him hot coffee and a roll. He did not look at her or thank her, but when he reached for his coffee he saw that there were two cups, and two hot croissants.

"Hey, Milos," he said in a rusty voice. "Breakfast time."

Design by David Bullen
Typeset in Mergenthaler Goudy Olde Style
by Harrington-Young
Printed by Maple-Vail
on acid-free paper